DYNA

Mesa Falls

The Key Players

Mesa Falls Ranch, Montana's premier luxury corporate retreat, got its start when a consortium bought the property.

The Owners

Weston Rivera, rancher

Miles Rivera, rancher

Gage Striker, investment banker

Desmond Pierce, casino resort owner

Alec Jacobsen, game developer

Jonah Norlander, technology company CEO

What do the owners have in common?

They all went to Dowdon School, where they were students of the late Alonzo Salazar.

The Salazars

Alonzo Salazar (dec.), retired teacher at Dowdon School, CEO of Salazar Media

Devon Salazar, copresident, Salazar Media, Alonzo's son

Marcus Salazar, copresident, Salazar Media, Alonzo's son, Devon's half brother

As these key players converge, dark secrets come to light in Big Sky Country...

Where family loyalties and passions collide...

"I need to be sure you want to stay."

Miles's breathing was harsh. "Tell me, Chiara."

"I've never felt the way you're making me feel tonight," Chiara confided. "But I've always wanted to. So, yes, I'm staying. I have to see what I've been missing all the years I chose work over...fun."

"It's going to be more than fun."

"Promise?"

"If you make me a promise in return."

"What is it?"

"I get a date after this. One where you'll tell me why you've chosen work over fun for far too long."

Her conscience stabbed her. Miles would probably hate her when he found out why she'd come. He'd never look at her the same way again—with heat and hunger in his eyes.

"Deal," she told him simply, knowing he'd never follow through on a date once he understood.

He breathed his agreement over her lips. "Deal."

* * *

The Rancher by Joanne Rock is part of the Dynasties: Mesa Falls series.

JOANNE ROCK

THE RANCHER

HARLEQUIN

DESIRE

To the Rockettes,
for keeping me company
while I write.

HARLEQUIN®
DESIRE™

Recycling programs
for this product may
not exist in your area.

ISBN-13: 978-1-335-23266-3

The Rancher

Copyright © 2021 by Joanne Rock

This edition published by arrangement with Harlequin Books S.A.

For questions and comments about the quality of this book,
please contact us at CustomerService@Harlequin.com.

Harlequin Enterprises ULC
22 Adelaide St. West, 40th Floor
Toronto, Ontario M5H 4E3, Canada
www.Harlequin.com

Printed in U.S.A.

Dear Reader,

Rancher Miles Rivera seemed like the last man in Montana who would have his head turned by a social media star. So it made me smile that Chiara Campagna is the woman to spin his life upside down when she comes to Mesa Falls looking for answers about her long lost friend who was once Miles's classmate.

Welcome back to Mesa Falls, where old secrets are simmering into new scandals for the friends who own a Montana luxury ranch. Miles and Chiara turn up the heat when he catches her red-handed in his office. She's in town only to uncover his secrets, but soon he's uncovering her instead. When danger threatens her, however, Miles is more determined than ever to keep her close.

I hope you're enjoying the series. Be sure to look for the exciting conclusion next month when *The Heir* comes to town.

Happy reading,

Joanne Rock

Joanne Rock credits her decision to write romance after a book she picked up during a flight delay engrossed her so thoroughly that she didn't mind at all when her flight was delayed two more times. Giving her readers the chance to escape into another world has motivated her to write over eighty books for a variety of Harlequin series.

Books by Joanne Rock

Harlequin Desire

Dynasties: Mesa Falls

The Rebel
The Rival
Rule Breaker
Heartbreaker
The Rancher

Texas Cattleman's Club: Inheritance

Her Texas Renegade

Visit her Author Profile page at Harlequin.com, or joannerock.com, for more titles.

You can also find Joanne Rock on Facebook, along with other Harlequin Desire authors, at Facebook.com/harlequindesireauthors!

One

Chiara Campagna slipped into her host's office and silently closed the heavy oak door, leaving the raucous party behind. Breathing in the scents of good bourbon and leather, she held herself very still in the darkened room while she listened for noise outside in the hallway to indicate if anyone had followed her.

When no sounds came through besides the pop song people danced to in the living room of Miles Rivera's spacious Montana vacation home, Chiara released a pent-up breath and debated whether or not to switch on a lamp. On the one hand, a light showing under the door might signal to someone passing by that the room was occupied when it shouldn't be. On the other, if someone found her by herself snooping around in the dark, she'd be raising significant suspicions that wouldn't be easy to talk her way around.

As a prominent Los Angeles-based social media influencer, Chiara had a legitimate reason to be at the party given by the Mesa Falls Ranch owners to publicize their environmental good works. But she had no legitimate reason to be *here*—in Miles Rivera's private office—snooping for secrets about his past.

She twisted the knob on the wall by the door, and recessed lighting cast a warm glow over the heavy, masculine furnishings. Dialing back the wattage with the dimmer, she left it just bright enough to see her way around the gray leather sofa and glass-topped coffee table to the midcentury modern desk. Her silver metallic dress, a gorgeous gown with an asymmetrical hem and thigh-high slit to show off her legs, moved around her with a soft rustle as she headed toward the sideboard with its decanter full of amber-colored liquid. She set aside her tiny silver handbag, then poured two fingers' worth into one of the glasses beside the decanter. If anyone discovered her, the drink would help explain why she'd lingered where she most definitely did not belong.

"What secrets are you hiding, Miles?" she asked a framed photo of her host, a flattering image of an already handsome man. In the picture, he stood in front of the guest lodge with the five other owners of Mesa Falls Ranch. It was one of the few photos she'd seen of all six of them together.

Each successful in his own right, the owners

were former classmates from a West Coast boarding school close to the all-girls' academy Chiara had attended. At least until her junior year, when her father lost his fortune and she'd been booted into public school. It would have been no big deal, really, if not for the fact that the public school had no art program. Her dreams of attending a prestigious art university to foster her skills with collage and acrylic paint faltered and died. Sure, she'd parlayed her limited resources into fame and fortune as a beauty influencer thanks to social media savvy and—in part— to her artistic sensibilities. But being an Instagram star wasn't the same as being an artist.

Not that it mattered now, she reminded herself, lingering on the photograph of Miles's too-handsome face. He stood flanked by casino resort owner Desmond Pierce and game developer Alec Jacobsen. Miles's golden, surfer looks were a contrast to Desmond's European sophistication and Alec's stubbled, devil-may-care style. All six men were wealthy and successful in their own right. Mesa Falls was the only business concern they shared.

A project that had something to do with the ties forged back in their boarding school days. A project that should have included Zach Eldridge, the seventh member of the group, who'd died under mysterious circumstances. The boy she'd secretly loved.

A cheer from the party in the living room reminded Chiara she needed to get a move on if she wanted to accomplish her mission. Steeling herself with a sip of the aged bourbon, she turned away from the built-in shelves toward the desk, then tapped the power button on the desktop computer. Any twinge of guilt she felt over invading Miles's privacy was mitigated by her certainty the Mesa Falls Ranch owners knew more than they were telling about Zach's death fourteen years ago. She hadn't been sure of it until last Christmas, when a celebrity guest of the ranch had revealed a former mentor to the ranch owners had anonymously authored a book that brought the men of Mesa Falls into the public spotlight.

And rekindled Chiara's need to learn the truth about what had happened to Zach while they were all at school together.

When the desktop computer prompted her to type in a passcode, Chiara crossed her fingers, then keyed in the same four numbers she'd seen Miles Rivera code into his phone screen earlier in the evening while ostensibly reaching past him for a glass of champagne. The generic photo of a mountain view on the screen faded into the more businesslike background of Miles's desktop with its neatly organized ranch files.

"Bingo." She quietly celebrated his lack of high tech cyber security on his personal device since she'd just exhausted the extent of her code-cracking abilities.

"Z-A-C-H." She spoke the letters aloud as she typed them into the search function.

A page full of results filled the screen. Her gaze roved over them. Speed-reading file names, she realized most of the files were spreadsheets; they seemed to be earnings reports. None used Zach's name in the title, indicating the references to him were within the files themselves.

Her finger hovered over a promising entry when the doorknob turned on the office door. Scared of getting caught, she jammed the power button off on the computer.

Just in time to look up and see Miles Rivera standing framed in the doorway.

Dressed in a custom-cut tuxedo that suited his lean runner's build perfectly, he held his phone in one hand before silently tucking it back in his jacket pocket. In the low light, his hair looked more brown than dark blond, the groomed bristles around his jaw and upper lip decidedly sexy. He might be a rancher, normally overseeing Rivera Ranch, a huge spread in central California, yet he was always well-dressed anytime the Mesa Falls owners were in the news cycle for their efforts to bring awareness to sustainable ranching practices. His suits were always tailored and masculine at the same time. Her blog followers would approve. She certainly approved of his blatant sexiness and comfort in his own skin, even though she was scared he was about to have her tossed out of his vacation home on the Mesa Falls property for snooping.

His blue eyes zeroed in on her with laser focus. Missing nothing.

Guilty heart racing, Chiara reached for her bourbon and lifted it to her lips slowly, hoping her host couldn't spot the way her hand shook from his position across the room.

"You caught me red-handed." She sipped too much of the drink, the strong spirit burning her throat the whole way down while she struggled to maintain her composure.

"At what, exactly?" Miles quirked an eyebrow, his expression impossible to read.

Had he seen her shut off the computer? She only had an instant to decide how to play this.

"Helping myself to your private reserves." She lifted the cut-crystal tumbler, as if to admire the amber contents in the light. "I only slipped in here to escape the noise for a few minutes, but when I saw the decanter, I hoped you wouldn't mind if I helped myself."

She waited for him to call her out for the lie. To accuse her of spying on him. Her heartbeat sounded so loud in her ears she thought for sure he must hear it, too.

He inclined his head briefly before shutting the door behind him, then striding closer. "You're my guest. You're welcome to whatever you like, Ms. *Campagna*."

She sensed an undercurrent in the words. Something off in the slight emphasis on her name. Because he knew she was lying? Because he remembered a time when that hadn't been her name? Or maybe due to the simple fact that he didn't seem to like her. She had enough of an empath's sensibilities to recognize when someone looked down on her career. She suspected Miles Rivera was the kind of man to pigeonhole her as frivolous because she posted beauty content online.

As if making women feel good about themselves was a waste of time.

"You're not a fan of mine," she observed lightly, sidling from behind his desk to pace the length of the room, pretending to be interested in the titles of books on the built-in shelves lining the back wall. "Is it because of my profession? Or does it have more to do with me invading your private domain and stealing some bourbon? It's excellent, by the way."

"It's a limited edition." He unbuttoned his jacket as he reached the wet bar, then picked up the decanter to pour a second glass, his diamond cufflink winking in the overhead lights as he poured. "Twenty-five years old. Single barrel. But I meant what I said. You're welcome to my hospitality. Including my bourbon."

Pivoting on his heel, he took two steps in her direction, then paused in front of his desk to lean against it. For a moment, she panicked that he would be able to feel that the computer was still warm. Or that the internal fan of the machine still spun after she'd shut it off.

But he merely sipped his drink while he observed her. He watched her so intently that she almost wondered if he recognized her from a long-ago past. In the few times they'd met socially, Miles had never made the connection between Chiara Campagna, social media star, and Kara Marsh, the teenager who'd been in love with Miles's roommate at school, Zach Eldridge. The old sense of loss flared inside her, spurring her to turn the conversation in a safer direction.

"I noticed you neatly sidestepped the matter of my profession." She set her tumbler on a granite-topped cabinet beside a heavy wire sculpture of a horse with a golden-yellow eye.

He paused, taking his time to answer. The sounds of the party filtered through to the dim home office. One dance tune blended seamlessly into another thanks to the famous DJ of the moment, and voices were raised to be heard over the music. When Miles met her gaze again, there was something calculating in his expression.

"Maybe I envy you a job that allows you to travel the globe and spend your nights at one party after another." He lifted his glass in a mock salute. "Clearly, you're doing something right."

Irritation flared.

"You wouldn't be the first person to assume I lead a charmed life of leisure, full of yachts and champagne, because of what I choose to show the world on social media." She bristled at his easy dismissal of all the hard work it had taken to carve herself a place in a crowded market.

"And yet, here you are." He gestured expansively, as if to indicate his second home on the exclusive Mesa Falls property. "Spending another evening with Hollywood celebrities, world-class athletes and a few heavyweights from the music industry. Life can't be all bad, can it?"

In her agitation, she took another drink of the bourbon, though she still hadn't learned her lesson to sip carefully. The fire down her throat should have warned her that she was letting this arrogant man get under her skin.

Considering her earlier fears about being caught spying, maybe she should have just laughed off his assumption that she had a shallow lifestyle and excused herself from the room. But resentment burned fast and hot.

"And yet, you're at the same party as me." She took a step closer to him before realizing it. Before acknowledging her own desire to confront him. To somehow douse the smug look in his blue eyes. "Don't you consider attendance part of your job, not just something you do for fun?"

"I'm the host representing Mesa Falls." His broad shoulders straightened at her approach, though he didn't move from his position leaning his hip against the desk. "Of course it's a work obligation. If I didn't have to take a turn being the face of Mesa Falls tonight, I would be back at my own place, Rivera Ranch."

His voice had a raspy quality to it that teased along her nerve endings in a way that wasn't at all unpleasant. He was nothing like the men who normally populated her world—men who understood the beauty and entertainment industries. There was something earthy and real about Miles Rivera underneath the tailored garments, something that compelled her to get closer to all those masculine, rough edges.

"And I'm representing my brand as well. It's no less a work obligation for me."

"Right." He shook his head, an amused smile playing at his lips, his blue eyes darkening a few shades. "More power to you for creating a brand that revolves around long-wearing lipstick and international fashion shows."

This view of her work seemed so unnecessarily dismissive that she had to wonder if he took potshots as a way to pay her back for invading his office. She couldn't imagine how he could rationalize his behavior any other way, but she forced herself to keep her cool in spite of his obvious desire to get a rise from her.

"I'm surprised a man of your business acumen would hold views so narrow-minded and superficial." She shrugged with deliberate carelessness, though she couldn't stop herself from glaring daggers at him. Or taking another step closer to hammer home her point. "Especially since I'm sure you recognize that work like mine requires me to be a one-woman content creator, marketing manager, finance director and admin. Not to mention committing endless hours to build a brand you write off as fluff."

Maybe what she'd said resonated for him, because the condescension in his expression gave way to something else. Something hotter and more complex. At the same moment, she realized that she'd arrived a foot away from him. Closer than she'd meant to come.

She couldn't have said which was more unnerving: the sudden lifting of a mental barrier between them that made Miles Rivera seem more human, or her physical proximity to a man who...stirred something inside her. Good or bad, she couldn't say, but she most definitely didn't want to deal with magnified emotions right now. Let alone the sudden burst of heat she felt just being near him.

Telling herself the jittery feelings were a combination of justified anger and residual anxiety from her snooping mission, Chiara reached for her silver purse on the desk. Her hand came close to his thigh for an instant before she snatched up the handbag.

She didn't look back as she stalked out the office door.

Still shaken by his unexpected encounter with Chiara Campagna, Miles made a dismal effort to mingle with his guests despite the loud music, the crowd that struck him as too young and entitled, and the text messages from the other Mesa Falls Ranch owners that kept distracting him. Trapped in his oversize great room that took "open concept" to a new level of monstrosity, he leaned against the curved granite-topped cabinetry that provided a low boundary between the dining area and seating around a stone fireplace that took up one entire wall. Open trusswork in the cathedral ceilings added to the sense of space, while the hardwood floor made for easy dancing as the crowd enjoyed the selections of the DJ set up near the open staircase.

Miles nodded absently at whatever the blonde pop singer standing next to him was saying about her reluctance to go back on tour, his thoughts preoccupied by another woman.

A certain raven-haired social media star who seemed to captivate every man in the room.

Miles's gaze followed Chiara as she posed for a photo with two members of a boy band in front of a wall of red flowers brought into the great room for the party. He couldn't take his eyes off her feminine curves draped in that outrageous liquid silver dress she wore. Hugged between the two young men, her gown reflected the flashes of multiple camera phones as several other guests took surreptitious photos. And while the guys around her only touched her in polite and socially acceptable ways, Miles still fought an urge to wrest her away from them. A ludicrous reaction, and totally out of character for him.

Then again, *everything* about his reaction to the wildly sexy Chiara was out of character. Since when was he the kind of guy to disparage what someone else did for a living? He'd regretted his flippant dismissal of her work as soon as he'd said the words, recognizing them as a defense mechanism he had no business articulating. There was something about her blatant appeal that slid past his reserve. The woman was like fingernails down his back, inciting response. Desire, yes. But there was more to it than that. He didn't trust the femme fatale face she presented to the world, or the way she used her femininity in an almost mercenary way to build her name. She reminded him of a woman from his past that he'd rather forget. But that wasn't fair, since Chiara wasn't Brianna. Without a doubt, he owed Chiara an apology before she left tonight.

Even though she'd definitely been on his computer when he'd entered his office earlier. He'd seen the blue glow of the screen reflected on her face before she'd scrambled to shut it down.

"How do you know Chiara Campagna?" the woman beside him asked, inclining her head so he could hear her over the music.

He hadn't been following the conversation, but Chiara's name snagged his focus, and he tore his gaze away from the beauty influencer who'd become a household name to stare down at the earnest young pop singer beside him.

He was only on site at Mesa Falls Ranch to oversee things for the owners for a few weeks. His real life back at Rivera Ranch in central California never brought him into contact with the kind of people on the guest list tonight, but the purpose of this party—

to promote the green ranching mission of Mesa Falls by spreading the word among celebrities who could use their platforms to highlight the environmental effort—was a far cry from the routine cattle raising and grain production he was used to. Just like his modern marvel of a home in Mesa Falls bore little resemblance to the historic Spanish-style main house on Rivera Ranch.

"I don't know her at all," Miles returned after a moment. He tried to remember the pop singer's name. She had a powerful voice despite her petite size, her latest single landing in the top ten according to the notes the ranch's publicist had given him about the guests. "But I assume she cares about Mesa Falls's environmental mission. No doubt she has a powerful social media platform that could help our outreach."

The singer laughed as she lifted her phone to take a picture of her own, framing Chiara and the two boy band members in her view screen. "Is that why we're all here tonight? Because of the environment?"

Frowning, he remembered the real reason for this particular party. While the green ranching practices they used were touted every time they hosted an event, tonight's party had a more important agenda. Public interest in Mesa Falls had spiked since the revelations that the owners' high school teacher and friend, Alonzo Salazar, had been the author behind the career-ending tell-all *Hollywood Newlyweds*. In fact, the news story broke at a gala here over Christmas. It had also been revealed that Alonzo had spent a lot of time at Mesa Falls before his death, his association with the ranch owners drawing speculation about his involvement with the business.

Tonight, the partners hoped to put an end to the rumors and tabloid interest by revealing the profits from *Hollywood Newlyweds* had gone toward Alonzo Salazar's humanitarian work around the globe. They'd hoped the announcement would put an end to the media interest in the Mesa Falls owners and discourage newshounds from showing up at the ranch. There'd been a coordinated press release of the news at the start of the party, a toast to the clearing of Alonzo's good name early in the evening, and a media room had been set up off the foyer with information about Alonzo's charitable efforts for reporters.

But there was something the owners weren't saying. While it was true a share of the book profits had benefited a lot of well-deserving people, a larger portion had gone to a secret beneficiary, and no one could figure out why.

"So the threat of global warming didn't bring you here tonight," Miles responded with a self-deprecating smile, trying to get back on track in his host duties. He watched as Chiara left behind the band members for one of the Mesa Falls partners—game developer Alec Jacobsen—who wanted a photo with her. "What did? A need to escape to Montana for a long weekend?"

He ground his teeth together at the friendly way

Alec placed his hand on the small of Chiara's back. Miles remembered the generous cutout in her dress that left her completely bare in that spot. Her hair shimmered in the overhead lights as she brushed the long waves over one shoulder.

"Honestly? I hoped to meet Chiara," the singer gushed enthusiastically. "Will you excuse me? Maybe I can get a photo with her, too."

Miles gladly released her from the conversation, chagrined to learn that his companion had been as preoccupied with Chiara as he was. What must life be like for the influencer, who'd achieved a different level of fame from the rest of the crowd—all people who were highly accomplished in their own right?

Pulling out his phone, Miles checked to see if his friend and fellow ranch owner, Gage Striker, had responded to a text he'd sent an hour ago. Gage should have been at the party long ago.

Miles had sent him a text earlier:

How well do you know Chiara Campagna? Found her in my study and I would swear she was riffling through my notes. Looking for something.

Gage had finally answered:

Astrid and Jonah have known her forever. She's cool.

Miles knew fellow partner Jonah Norlander had made an early exit from the party with his wife, Astrid, so Miles would have to wait to check with him. Shoving the phone back in the pocket of his tuxedo, Miles bided his time until he could speak to Chiara again. He would apologize, first and foremost. But then, he needed to learn more about her.

Because she hadn't just been snooping around his computer in his office earlier. She'd been there on a mission. And she hadn't covered her trail when she'd rushed to close down his screen.

Somehow, Chiara Campagna knew about Zach. And Miles wasn't letting her leave Mesa Falls until he figured out how.

Two

Chiara grooved on the dance floor to an old disco tune, surrounded by a dozen other guests and yet— thankfully—all by herself. She'd spent time snapping photos with people earlier, so no one entered her personal dance space while she took a last glance around the party she should have left an hour ago.

Normally, she kept a strict schedule at events like this, making only brief appearances at all but the biggest of social engagements. The Met Gala might get a whole evening, or an Oscar after-party. But a gathering hosted by a Montana rancher in a thinly disguised PR effort to turn attention away from the Alonzo Salazar book scandal?

She should have been in and out in fifty minutes

once her spying mission in Miles Rivera's office had proven a bust. Finding out something about Zach had been her real motive for attending, yet she'd lingered long after she'd failed in that regard. And she knew the reason had something to do with her host. She knew because she found herself searching him out in the crowd, her eyes scanning the darkened corners of the huge great room hoping for a glimpse of him.

Entirely foolish of her.

Annoyed with herself for the curiosity about a man who, at best, was keeping secrets about Zach and at worst thought her work shallow and superficial, she was just about to walk off the dance floor when he reentered the room. His sudden presence seemed to rearrange the atoms in the air, making it more charged. Electrified.

For a moment, he didn't notice her as he read something on his phone, and she took the opportunity to look her fill while unobserved. She was curious what it was about him that held her attention. His incredibly fit physique? Certainly with his broad shoulders he cut through the guests easily enough, his size making him visible despite the crowd around him. Or maybe it was the way he held himself, with an enviable confidence and authority that implied he was a man who solved problems and took care of business. But before she could explore other facets of his appeal, his gaze lifted from his device to land squarely on her.

Almost as if he'd known the whole time she'd been watching him.

A keen awareness took hold as she flushed all over. Grateful for the dim lighting in the great room, she took some comfort in the fact that at least he wouldn't see how he affected her. Even if he had caught her staring.

Abruptly, she stepped out of the throng of dancers with brisk efficiency, determined to make her exit. Heels clicking purposefully on the hardwood, she moved toward the foyer, texting her assistant that she was ready to leave. But just as the other woman appeared at her side to gather their entourage, Miles intercepted Chiara.

"Don't go." His words, his serious tone, were almost as much of a surprise as his hand catching hers lightly in his own. "Can we speak privately?"

It might have been satisfying to say something cutting now in return for the way he'd behaved with her earlier. To hold her head high and march out his front door into the night. She looked back and forth between Miles and her assistant, Jules Santor, who was busy on her phone assembling vehicles for the return to their nearby hotel. But the reason Chiara had come here tonight was more important than her pride, and if there was any chance she could still wrest some clue about Zach's death from Miles after all this time, she couldn't afford to indulge the impulse.

"On second thought," she told Jules, a very tall

former volleyball player who turned heads everywhere she went, "feel free to take the rest of the evening off. I'm going to stay a bit longer."

Jules bit her lip, her thumbs paused midtext as she glanced around the party. "Are you sure you'll be okay? Do you want me to leave a car for you?"

"I'll be fine. I'll text if I need a ride," Chiara assured her before returning her attention to whatever Miles had in mind.

At her nod, he guided her toward the staircase behind the dining area, one set of steps leading to an upper floor and another to a lower. He took her downstairs, never relinquishing her hand. A social nicety, maybe, because of her sky-high heels, long gown and the open stairs. Yet his touch made her pulse quicken.

When they reached the bottom floor, there was a small bar and a mahogany billiards table with a few guys engaged in a game. He led her past a smaller living area that was dark except for a fire in the hearth, through a set of double doors into a huge room with a pool and floor-to-ceiling windows on three sides. Natural stonework surrounded the entire pool deck, making it look like a grotto complete with a small waterfall from a raised hot tub. The water was illuminated from within, and landscape lights showcased a handful of plantings and small trees.

"This is beautiful." She paused as they reached two easy chairs flanking a cocktail table by the windows that overlooked the backyard and the Bitter-root River beyond.

Withdrawing her hand from his, she took the seat he gestured toward while he made himself comfortable in the other.

"Thank you." He pulled his gaze from her long enough to look over the pool area. "I keep meaning to come here during the summer when I could actually open all the doors and windows and feel the fresh air circulating."

"You've never visited this house during the summer?" She wondered if she misunderstood him. The house where he was hosting tonight's party was at least fourteen thousand square feet.

"I'm rarely ever in Montana." His blue eyes found hers again as he leaned forward in the wingback, elbows propped on his knees. "Normally, my brother oversees Mesa Falls while I maintain Rivera Ranch, but Weston had his hands full this year, so I'm helping out here for the month." His jaw flexed. "I realize I did a poor job in my hosting duties earlier this evening, however."

Surprised he would admit it, she felt her brows lift but waited for him to continue. The sounds of the game at the billiards table drifted through the room now and then, but for the most part, the soft gurgle of the waterfall drowned out the noise of the party. The evening was winding down anyhow.

"I had no right to speak disparagingly of your

work, and I apologize." He hung his head for a moment as he shook it, appearing genuinely regretful. "I don't know what I was thinking, but it was completely inappropriate."

"Agreed." She folded her fingers together, hands in her lap, as she watched him. "Apology accepted."

He lifted his head, that amused smile she remembered from earlier flitting around his lips again. "You're an unusual woman, Chiara Campagna."

"How so?" Crossing her legs, she wished she didn't feel a flutter inside at the sound of her name on his lips. She couldn't have walked away from this conversation if she tried.

She was curious why he'd sought her out for a private audience again. Had she been in his thoughts as much as he'd been in hers over the last hour? Not that it should matter. She hadn't decided to stay longer at the party because he made her entire body flush hot with a single look. No, she was here now because Miles knew something about Zach's death, and getting to know Miles might help her find out what had really happened.

"Your candor, for one thing." He slid a finger beneath his bow tie, expertly loosening it a fraction.

Her gaze tracked to his throat, imagining the taste of his skin at the spot just above his collar. It was easier to indulge in a little fantasy about Miles than it was to reply to his opinion of her, which was so very wrong. She'd been anything but truthful with him this evening.

"I appreciated the way you explained your job to me when I made a crack about it," he continued, unbuttoning his tuxedo jacket and giving her a better view of the white shirt stretching taut across his chest and abs. He looked very…fit. "I had no idea how much work was involved."

Her gaze lingered on his chest as she wondered how much more unbuttoning he might do in her presence tonight. She didn't know where all this physical attraction was coming from, but she wished she could put the lid back on it. Normally, she didn't think twice about pursuing relationships, preferring to focus on her work. But then, men didn't usually tempt her to this degree. The awareness was beyond distracting when she needed to be smart about her interaction with him. With an effort, she tried to focus on their conversation.

"I'm sure plenty of jobs look easier from the outside. You're a rancher, for example, and I'm sure that amounts to more than moving cattle from one field to the next, but that's really all I know about it."

"Yet whereas you have the good sense to simply admit that, I made presumptuous wisecracks because I didn't understand your work." He studied her for a long moment before he spoke again. "I appreciate you being here tonight. I do recognize that our ranch party probably wouldn't be on your list of social engagements if not for your friendship with Jonah Norlander's wife, Astrid."

"Astrid is one of my closest friends," she said, wary of going into too much detail about her connections to the Mesa Falls partners and their spouses. But at least she was telling the truth about Astrid. The Finnish former supermodel had caused Chiara's career to skyrocket, simply by posting enthusiastic comments on Chiara's social media content. Because of her friend, she'd gone from an unknown to a full-blown influencer practically overnight. "As someone who doesn't have much family, I don't take for granted the few good friends I have in my life."

Another reason she planned to honor Zach's memory. She counted him among the people who'd given her the creative and emotional boost she'd needed to find her professional passion.

"Wise woman." Miles nodded his agreement. "I guess you could say I'm here tonight because of my good friends, too. I do have family, but I don't mind admitting I like my friends better."

His grin was unrepentant, giving his blue eyes a wicked light.

"What about Weston?" She wondered what he thought of his younger brother, who held a stake in Mesa Falls with him.

"We have our moments," he told her cryptically, his lips compressing into a thin line as some dark thought raced across his expression.

"Does owning the ranch together make you closer with him?"

One eyebrow arched. "It does."

His clipped answer made her hesitate to probe further. But she couldn't stop herself from asking, "If you're close to the other Mesa Falls owners, why don't you spend more time here? I know you said you run Rivera Ranch, but why build this huge, beautiful house if you didn't ever plan on making time to be in Montana?"

She wondered what kept him away. Yes, she was curious if it had anything to do with Zach. But she couldn't deny she wanted to know more about Miles. With luck, that knowledge would help her keep her distance from this far-too-sexy man.

He took so long to answer that she thought maybe he'd tell her it was none of her business. He watched the spillover from the hot tub where it splashed into the pool below, and she realized the sounds had faded from the other room; the billiard game had ended.

"Maybe I was feeling more optimistic when we bought the land." He met her gaze. "Like having this place would bring us together more. But for the most part, it's just another asset we manage."

Puzzled why that would be, she drew in a breath to tease out the reason, but he surprised her into silence when his hand landed on her wrist.

"Isn't it my turn to ask you something?" Mild amusement glinted in his eyes again.

Her belly tightened at his attention, his touch. There was a potent chemistry lurking between them, and she wanted to exercise extreme caution not to stir it any further. But it was incredibly tempting to see what would happen if she acted on those feelings. Too late, she realized that her pulse leaped right underneath the place where his hand rested. His thumb skated over the spot with what might pass for idleness to anyone observing them, but that slow caress felt deliberate to her.

As if he wanted to assess the results of his touch.

"What?" she prodded him, since the suspense of the moment was killing her.

Or maybe it was the awareness. She was nearly brought to her knees by physical attraction.

"I saw you dancing alone upstairs." His voice took on that low, raspy quality that sent her thoughts to sexy places.

She remembered exactly what she'd been thinking about when he'd caught her eye earlier. She would not lick her lips, even though they suddenly felt dry.

"That's not a question," she managed, willing her pulse to slow down under the stroke of his thumb.

"It made me wonder," he continued as if she hadn't spoken. "Would you like to dance with me instead?"

The question, like his touch, seemed innocuous on the surface. But she knew he wasn't just asking her to dance. She *knew*.

That should have given her pause before she answered. But she gave him the only possible response.

"I'd like that." She pushed the words past the sudden lump in her throat. "Very much."

Even before he'd asked her to be his dance partner, Miles knew the party upstairs had ended and that this would be a private dance.

The Mesa Falls PR team excelled at keeping events on schedule, and the plan had been to move the late-night guests into the media room to distribute gift bags at midnight. His public hosting duties were officially done.

His private guest was now his only concern.

Which was a good thing, since he couldn't have taken his eyes off her if he tried. He needed to figure out what she was up to, after all. What would it hurt to act on the attraction since he had to keep track of what she was doing anyway? Keep your friends close and your enemies closer. Wherever Chiara ended up on the spectrum, he'd have his bases covered.

Helping her to her feet, he kept hold of her hand as he steered her toward the billiards room, now empty. Stopping there, he flipped on the speaker system tucked behind the bar, then dimmed the lights and pressed the switch for the gas fireplace at the opposite end of the room. Her green eyes took in the changes before her gaze returned to him.

"Aren't we going upstairs?" she asked while the opening refrain of a country love song filled the air.

Miles shrugged off his tuxedo jacket and laid it over one of the chairs at the bar. If he was fortunate enough to get to feel her hands on him tonight, he didn't want extraneous layers of clothes between them.

"The DJ is done for the night." He led her to the open floor near the pool table and pulled her closer to him, so they faced one another, still holding hands. He waited to take her into his arms until he was certain she wanted this. "I thought if we stayed down here we'd be out of the way of the catering staff while they clean up."

"I didn't realize the party was over." She didn't seem deterred, however, because she laid her free hand on his shoulder, the soft weight of her touch stirring awareness that grew by the minute. He was glad he'd ditched his jacket, especially when her fingers flexed against the cotton of his shirt, her fingernails lightly scratching the fabric.

"It's just us now." He couldn't help the way his voice lowered, maybe because he wanted to whisper the words into her ear. But he still didn't draw her to him. "Are you sure you want to stay?"

"It's too late to retract your offer, Miles Rivera." She lifted their joined hands, positioning them. "I'll have that dance, please."

Damn, but she fascinated him.

With far more pleasure than a dance had ever inspired in him, he slid his free hand around Chiara's waist. He took his time to savor the feel of her beneath his palm, the temperature of her skin making her dress's lightweight metallic fabric surprisingly warm. Sketching a touch from her hip to her spine, he settled his hand in the small of her back where the skin was bare, then used his palm to draw her within an inch of him.

Her pupils dilated until there was only a dark green ring around them.

"That's what I hoped you'd say." He swayed with her to the mournful, longing sound of steel guitars, breathing in her bright, citrusy scent.

Counting down the seconds until he kissed her.

Because he had to taste her soon.

Not just for the obvious reasons, like that she was the sexiest woman he'd ever seen. But because Chiara had gotten to the heart of the loneliness he felt in this big Montana mansion every time he set foot in the state. With her questions and her perceptive gaze, she'd reminded him that Mesa Falls might be a testament to Zach Eldridge's life, but it remained a hollow tribute without their dead friend among them.

He'd hoped that ache would subside after they'd owned the property for a while. That Mesa Falls could somehow heal the emptiness, the pervasive sense of failure, that remained in him and his partners after they'd lost one of their own. But for Miles, who'd defined his whole life by trying to do the right thing, the consequences of not saving his friend were as jagged and painful as ever.

"Is everything okay?" Chiara asked him, her hand leaving his shoulder to land on his cheek, her words as gentle as her expression.

And damned if that didn't hurt, too.

He didn't want her sympathy. Not when her kiss would feel so much better.

With an effort, he shoved his demons off his back and refocused on this woman's lush mouth. Her petal-soft fingertips skimming along his jaw. Her hips hovering close enough to his to tantalize him with what he wanted most.

"Just wondering how long I can make this dance last without violating social conventions." He let his gaze dip to her lips before meeting her gaze again.

She hesitated, her fingers going still against his cheek. He could tell she didn't buy it. Then her hand drifted from his face to his chest.

"You're worried what I'll think about you?" she asked lightly, her forefinger circling below his collarbone.

The touch was a barely there caress, but it told him she wasn't in any hurry to leave. The knowledge made his heart slug harder.

"A host has certain obligations to the people he invites under his roof." He stopped swaying to the song and looked into her eyes.

He kept one hand on the small of her back, the other still entwined with hers.

"In that case—" Her voice was breathless, but her gaze was steady. Certain. "I think you're obligated to make sure I don't dance alone again tonight."

Three

She needed his kiss.

Craved it.

Chiara watched Miles as he seemed to debate the merits of continuing what he'd started. He was a deliberate, thoughtful man. But she couldn't wait much longer, not when she felt this edgy hunger unlike anything she'd felt before.

She simply knew she wanted him. Even if what was happening between them probably shouldn't.

Maybe the impatience was because she'd had very little romantic experience. In her late teens, she'd mourned Zach and wrestled with the mix of anxiety and depression that had come with his death. Her lifestyle had shifted, too, after her father went bankrupt and she'd been forced to change schools. Giving up her dream of going to an art school had changed her, forging her into a woman of relentless ambition with no time for romance.

Not that it had really mattered to her before, since she hadn't been impressed with the few relationships she'd had in the past. The explosive chemistry other women raved about had been more of a simmer for her, making her feel like she'd only been going through the motions with guys. But tonight, dancing with Miles in this huge, empty house now that all the party guests had gone home, she felt something much different.

Something had shifted between them this evening, taking them from cautiously circling enemies to charged magnets that couldn't stay apart. At least, that's how she felt. Like she was inexorably drawn to him.

Especially with his broad palm splayed across her back, his thumb and forefinger resting on her bare skin through the cutout in the fabric of her gown, the other fingers straying onto the curve of her ass. A touch that made her very aware of his hands and how much she wanted them all over her without the barrier of clothes.

Determined to overcome his scruples, or host obligations, or whatever it was that made him hesitate, Chiara lifted up on her toes. She was going to take this kiss, and whatever else he was offering, because she needed it. She'd worry about the repercussions in the morning. For now, she grazed her mouth over his. Gently. Experimentally.

Hopefully.

She breathed him in, a hint of smoky bourbon enticing her tongue to taste his lower lip.

The contact sparked through her in unexpected ways, leaping from one pulse point to the next until something hot flamed to life. Something new and exciting. And as much as she wanted to explore that, she hesitated, worried about compounding her subterfuge with this man by adding seduction into the mix. Or maybe she just feared she didn't have the necessary skills. Either way, she needed to be sure he wanted this, too.

Just when she was about to pull back, his fingers tangled in her hair, anchoring her to him and deepening the kiss. And every cell in her body cried out a resounding *yes*.

The heat erupted into a full-blown blaze as he took over. With one hand he drew her body against his, sealing them together, while he used the other to angle her face in a way that changed the trajectory of the kiss from sensual to fierce and hungry. She pressed her thighs together against the sudden ache there.

From just a kiss.

Her body thrilled to the new sensations even as her brain struggled to keep up with the onslaught. Her scalp tingled when he ran his fingers through her hair. Her nipples beaded, skin tightening everywhere. A soft, needy sound emanated from the back of her throat, and the noise seemed to spur him on. His arm banded her tighter, creating delicious friction between their bodies as he backed her into the pool table. She wanted to peel off her gown and climb all over him. She simply *wanted*.

Her hands went to his shirt, ready to strip away the barriers between them, her fingers taking in the warm strength of all that delectable male muscle as she worked the fastenings. He lifted her up, seating her on the pool table as he stepped between her knees, never breaking the kiss. The long slit in her silver gown parted, making the fabric slide away as it ceased to cover her. The feel of him against her *there*, his hips pressing into the cradle of her thighs, made her forget everything else. Her fingers fell away from the shirt fastenings as she raked in a gasp, sensation rocking her.

Miles edged back, his blue eyes now a deep, dark ultramarine as his gaze smoked over her, checking in with her.

"I need to be sure you want to stay." His breathing was harsh as he tipped his forehead to hers, his grip going slack so that his palms simply rested on her hips. "Tell me, Chiara."

She respected his restraint. His concern for her. Things had spiraled out of control in a hurry, but she didn't want to stop now, no matter how it might complicate things down the road. She wanted to know real passion. What it was like to be carried away on that wave of hot, twitchy, need-it-now hunger.

"I've never felt the way you're making me feel tonight," she confided in a low voice, her hands gripping the side rails of the table, her nails sinking into the felt nap. "But I've always wanted to. So yes, I'm staying. I have to see what I've been missing all the years I chose work over…fun."

His lips quirked at that last bit. He straightened enough to look into her eyes again. The flames from the fireplace cast his face half in shadow.

"It's going to be more than fun." His thumbs rubbed lightly where they rested on her hips, the certainty in his tone assuring her he knew how to give her everything she craved.

She resisted the urge to squeeze his hips between her thighs and lock her ankles so he couldn't leave her. "Promise?"

His fingers clenched reflexively, which made her think that she affected him as thoroughly as he was affecting her.

"If you make me a promise in return."

"What is it?" She would have agreed to almost anything to put his hands in motion again. To experience another mind-drugging kiss with the power to set her on fire. How did he do that?

"I get a date after this." He pressed his finger to her lips when she'd been about to agree, silencing her for a moment while she battled the urge to lick him there. "One where you'll tell me why you've chosen work over fun for far too long," he continued, removing his finger from her mouth so she could speak.

Her conscience stabbed her as Zach's face floated through her mind. She had no idea how she'd appeal to Miles for information about Zach in the aftermath of this. He'd probably hate her when he found out why she'd come to Montana in the first place. He'd never look at her the same way again—with heat and hunger in his eyes. Was it so wrong to chase the feelings Miles stirred inside her?

"Deal," she told him simply, knowing he'd never follow through on the request once he understood what had brought her here in the first place. Her fingers returned to the studs in his shirt, wanting the barriers between them gone.

He tipped her chin up to meet his gaze before he breathed his agreement over her lips. "Deal."

His kiss seemed to seal the pact, and her fingers forgot how to work. All her thoughts scattered until there was only his tongue stroking hers, teasing wicked sensations that echoed over her skin, dialing up the heat. She shifted closer to him, wanting to be near the source of that warmth. He answered by bracketing her hips and tugging her forward to the edge of the table, pressing her against the rigid length beneath his fly.

She couldn't stifle the needy sound she made at the feel of him, the proof of his hunger pleasing her almost as much as having him right where she wanted him. Almost, anyway. A shiver rippled through her while he tugged the straps of her gown off her shoulders.

"I need to see you," he said as he broke the kiss, watching the metallic silver gown slide down her body.

The material teased her sensitive nipples as it fell, since she hadn't bothered to wear a bra. Miles's eyes locked on her body, and the peaks tightened almost painfully, her breath coming faster.

"And I need to *feel* you." She might not have a ton of romance experience, but she believed in voicing her needs. And damn it, she knew what she wanted. "Your hands, your body, your mouth. You pick."

His blue eyes were full of heat as they lifted to hers again. "Let's find a bed. Now."

He plucked her off the table and set her on her feet while she clutched enough of her gown to keep it from falling off. Holding her hand, Miles tugged her through the bar area and past an office to a bedroom with high wooden ceilings and lots of windows. She guessed it wasn't the master suite in a home like this, given its modest size and single closet, yet she glimpsed a pair of boots near the door and toiletries on the granite vanity of the attached bath.

Miles closed the door behind her, toed off his shoes, then made quick work of his shirt, tossing it on a built-in window seat.

She was about to ask why he was staying in a guest bedroom of his own home when he came toward her. The words dried up on her tongue at the sight of his purposeful stride.

When he reached her, he took the bodice she was clutching and let it fall to the floor, the heavy liquid silver pooling at her feet. Cool air touched her skin now that she was almost naked except for an ice-blue silk thong.

She didn't have long to feel the chill, however, as Miles pressed her body to his. Her breasts molded to his hard chest as his body radiated heat. He took his time wrapping her hair around his hand, lifting the heavy mass off her shoulders and watching it spill down his forearm.

"My hands, my body, my mouth." He parroted the words back to her, the rough sound of his voice letting her know how they'd affected him. "I pick all three."

Oh.

He kissed her throat and the crook behind her ear, then trailed his lips down to her shoulder, letting her feel his tongue and his teeth until she twined her limbs around him, wanting to be closer. He drew her with him to the bed, his hands tracing light touches up her arms, down her sides, under her breasts. When her calf bumped into the mattress, she dropped onto the gray duvet, pulling him down with her into the thick, downy embrace. She wanted to feel the weight of him against her, but he sat beside her on the edge of the bed instead, leaning down to unfasten the strap of her sequined sandal with methodical care.

A shiver went through her that had nothing to do with room temperature. When the first shoe fell away, he slid a warm palm down her other leg, lifting it to undo the tiny buckle on her other ankle. Once that shoe dropped onto the floor, he skimmed his hand back up her leg, circling a light touch behind her knee, then following the line of muscle in her thigh. Higher.

Higher.

She was on fire, desperate for more, by the time he pressed her back onto the bed. He followed her down, combing his fingers through her dark hair and kissing her neck, bracketing her body between his elbows where he propped himself over her. He kissed her jaw and down her neck, tracing a touch down the center of her breastbone, slowing but not stopping as he tracked lower. Lower.

Her pulse rushed as she inhaled sharply. She noticed he was breathing faster, too, his eyes watching the movement of his fingers as he reached the low waist of the ice-blue silk thong that still clung to her hips. As he slipped his fingers beneath the fabric, the brush of his knuckles made her stomach muscles clench, tension tightening as he stroked a touch right where she needed it. His gaze returned to her face as a ripple of pleasure trembled through her. She was already so close, on edge from wondering what would happen between them. Her release hovered as she held her breath.

He must have known. She didn't know how he could tell, but he leaned down to speak into her ear.

"You don't need to hold back." That deep, suggestive voice vibrated along her skin, evaporating any restraint. "There's no limit on how many times you can come."

His fingers stroked harder, and she flew apart. She gripped his wrist, whether to push him away or keep him there, she didn't know, but he didn't let go. Expertly, he coaxed every last shudder from her while waves of pleasure rocked through her. Only when she went still, her breathing slowing a fraction, did he slide off the bed.

She would have mourned the loss, but he shoved off his pants and boxers, reminding her how much more she had to look forward to. He disappeared into the bathroom for a moment but returned a moment later in all his delectable naked glory, condom in hand. Yet even as she tried to memorize the way he looked, to take in all the ways his muscles moved together so that she'd never forget it, she experienced a moment's trepidation. Just because he'd known how to touch her in a way that had made the earth move for her didn't mean she could return the favor.

But when he joined her on the bed, handing her the condom and letting her roll it in place, the worries faded. Having him next to her, covering her with all that warm male muscle as he kneed her legs apart to make room for himself, made it impossible to think about anything but this.

Him.

The most tantalizing encounter she'd ever had with a man.

He kissed her as he eased his way inside her, moving with her as easily as if they'd done this a thousand times before. Closing her eyes, she breathed in his cedarwood scent, letting the heat build between them again, hotter and stronger this time. The connection between them felt so real to her, even though she knew it could only be passion or chemistry, or whatever that nameless X-factor was that made for amazing sex.

Still, when she opened her eyes and found his intense gaze zeroed in on her, she could have sworn he'd seen deep inside her, past all the artifice that was her whole life and right down to the woman underneath. The thought robbed her of breath, stirring a hint of panic until he kissed her again, shifting on top of her in a way that created heart-stopping friction between their bodies.

He thrust again. Once. Twice.

And she lost all her bearings, soaring mindlessly into another release. This time, she brought him with her. She could feel him going still, his shout echoing hers, their bodies utterly in sync. For long moments, all she could do was breathe, dragging in long gulps of air while her heart galloped faster.

Eventually, everything slowed down again. Her

skin cooled as Miles rolled away, but he dragged a cashmere throw up from the base of the bed, covering them both. He pulled her against him, her back tucked against his chest, as he stroked her hair in the darkened room. Words failed her, and she was grateful that he didn't say anything, either. She was out of her depth tonight, but she wasn't ready to leave. The only solace she took was that he didn't seem to want her to go.

In the morning, she'd have to come clean about what she was doing here. She hoped he wouldn't hate her for sleeping with him after she'd tried spying on him. Chances seemed slim that he'd understand the truth—that the two things were entirely unrelated.

Who was she kidding? He'd never believe that.

Guilt and worry tightened in her belly.

"Whatever you're thinking about, stop," came Miles's advice in her ear, a warm reassurance she didn't deserve. "Just enjoy it while we can."

How had he known? Maybe he'd felt her tense. Either way, she didn't feel compelled to wreck what they'd just shared, so she let out a long breath and tucked closer to his warmth.

The morning—and all the consequences of her decision to stay—would come soon enough.

Miles awoke twice in the night.

The first time, he'd reached for the woman in his bed on instinct, losing himself in her all over again.

She'd been right there with him, touching him with the urgency of someone who didn't want to waste a second of this time together, as if she knew as well as he did that it wouldn't be repeated. The knowledge gave every kiss, every sigh a desperate need that only heightened how damned good it all felt.

The second time he'd opened his eyes, he'd felt her stirring beside him, her head tipping to his chest as if she belonged there. For some reason, that trust she would have never given him while awake seemed as much a gift as her body had been.

Another moment that he wouldn't be able to repeat.

So when daylight crept over the bed, he couldn't pretend that he felt no regrets. Not about what they'd shared, because Chiara cast a long shadow over every other woman he'd ever been with. No, he didn't regret what had happened. Only that the night was a memory now.

And that's what it had to remain.

He guessed Chiara knew as much, since the pillow next to his was empty. He heard the shower running and left some clothes for her in the dressing room outside the bathroom. The T-shirt and sweats with a drawstring would be huge on her, but a better alternative than her evening gown.

He grabbed cargoes and a Henley for himself before retreating to the pool to swim some laps and hit the shower there. Afterward he retreated to the kitchen to work on breakfast, making good use of the fresh tortillas from a local source his brother, Weston, had mentioned to him. While he and Wes had never been close, they shared a love for the food from growing up with their *abuela* Rosa's incredible cooking on Rivera Ranch. Miles scrambled eggs and browned the sausage, then chopped tomatoes and avocadoes. By the time Chiara appeared in the kitchen to help herself to coffee, the breakfast enchiladas were ready.

"Morning." She pulled down a mug from a hook over the coffee bar and set it on the granite. "I didn't mean to wake you."

At first look, there was something soft and vulnerable about her in the clothes he'd left for her. She'd rolled up the gray sweats to keep them from dragging on the floor; he saw she was wearing his gym socks. The dark blue T-shirt gaped around her shoulders, but she'd tucked a corner of the hem into the cinched waist of the sweats. Memories of their night together blindsided him, the need to pull her to him rising up again as inevitably as high tide.

Then she met his gaze, and any illusion of her vulnerability vanished. Her green eyes reflected a defensiveness that went beyond normal morning-after wariness. She appeared ready to sprint out of there at the first opportunity. Had her spying mission been a success the night before, so that she could afford to walk away from him now? He hadn't been aware that at least a part of him—and yeah, he knew which part—had hoped she'd stick around if she wanted to learn more about Mesa Falls.

Damn it. He needed to be smarter about this if he wanted to remain a step ahead of her.

"You didn't wake me," he finally replied as he grappled with how to put her at ease long enough to have a conversation about where things stood between them. "At home, I'm usually up before now." Gesturing toward the coffee station, he took the skillet off the burner. "Grab your cup and join me for breakfast."

He carried the dishes over to their place settings at the table for eight. The table felt big for two people, but he arranged things so he'd be sitting diagonally from her and could easily gauge her reaction to what he had to say.

Chiara bypassed the single-cup maker for the espresso machine, brewing a double shot. When she finished, she carried her mug over and lowered herself into one of the chairs.

"You didn't have to go to all this trouble." She held herself straight in the chair, her posture as tense as her voice.

What he couldn't figure out was why she was so nervous. Whatever preyed on her mind seemed weightier than next-day second thoughts. Was she thinking about whatever information she'd gleaned from his study during the party?

"It was no trouble." He lifted the top of the skillet to serve her. "Can I interest you in any?" At her hesitation, he continued, "I won't be offended either way."

Her eyes darted to his before she picked up her fork and slid an enchilada onto her plate. "It smells really good. Thank you."

He served himself afterward and dug in, debating how best to convince her to spend more time in Montana. He didn't want to leverage what happened between them unfairly—or twist her arm into keeping that date she'd promised him—but questions remained about what she was doing in his office the night before. If she knew about Zach, he needed to know how and why.

While he puzzled that out, however, Chiara set her fork down after a few bites.

"Miles, I can't in good conscience eat your food—which is delicious, by the way—when I haven't been honest with you." She blurted the words as if they'd been on the tip of her tongue for hours.

He slowly set aside his fork, wondering what she meant. Would she confess what she'd been doing in his office last night? Something else?

"I'm listening." He took in her ramrod-straight posture, the way she flicked a red-painted fingernail along the handle of the mug.

A breath whooshed from her lungs before she spoke again.

"I'm an old friend of Zach Eldridge's." The name of his dead friend on her lips sent a chill through him. "I came here last night to learn the truth about what happened to him."

Four

Miles didn't remember standing up from the table, but he must have after Chiara's startling announcement. Because the next thing he knew, he was staring out the kitchen window into a side yard and the Bitterroot River meandering in a bed of slushy ice. He felt ice on the inside, too, since numbing his feelings about his dead friend had always been a hell of a lot easier than letting them burn away inside him.

Snow blanketed the property, coating everything in white. Spring might be around the corner, but western Montana didn't know it today. Staring at the unbroken field of white helped him collect his thoughts enough to face her again.

"You knew Zach?" It had never crossed his mind

that she could have had a personal relationship with Zach even though he'd seen the search history on his computer. He'd assumed she'd heard an old rumor. If she'd known him, wouldn't she have come forward before now?

Zachary Eldridge had never talked about his life before his stint in a foster home near Dowdon School on the edge of the Ventana Wilderness in central California where the ranch owners had met. The way Zach had avoided the topic had broadcast all too clearly the subject was off-limits, and Miles had respected that. So he didn't think Chiara could have known him from that time. And he'd never heard rumors of her being in the foster system, making it doubtful she'd met him that way. Zach had been on a scholarship at their all-boys boarding school, a place she obviously hadn't attended.

"Dowdon School did events with Brookfield Academy." She clutched the espresso cup tighter, her gaze sliding toward the river-stone fireplace in the front room, though her expression had the blankness of someone seeing another place and time. Miles was familiar with the prestigious all-girls institution in close proximity to his alma mater. "I met Zach through the art program the summer before my sophomore year."

"You were at Brookfield?" Miles moved back toward the table, struggling to focus on the conversation—on her—no matter how much it hurt to remember the most painful time of his life. And yes, he was drawn to the sound of her voice and a desire to know her better.

He dropped back into his seat, needing to figure out how much she knew about Zach's death and the real motives behind her being in Mesa Falls all these years later.

"Briefly." She nodded her acknowledgment, her green eyes refocusing on him as he returned to the table. "I only attended for two years before my father lost everything in a bad investment and I had to leave Brookfield to go to public school."

Miles wondered why he hadn't heard of her connection to Zach or even to Brookfield. While he'd never sought out information about her, he would have thought her school affiliation would have been noted by the ranch's PR department when she was invited to Mesa Falls events.

Questions raced through his mind. How close had she been to Zach? Close enough to understand his mindset the weekend he'd died?

A hollow ache formed in his chest.

"How well did you know him?" He regretted the demanding sound of the question as soon as it left his lips, unsure how it would come across. "That is, I'm interested how you could make friends during a summer program. The school staff was strict about prohibiting visits between campuses."

Her lips quirked unexpectedly, her eyes lifting to meet his. "Zach wasn't afraid to bend rules when it suited him, though, was he?"

Miles couldn't help a short bark of laughter as the truth of that statement hit home. "'Rules are for people with conventional minds,' he once told me."

Chiara sat back in her chair, some of her rigid tension loosening as warmth and fondness lit her gaze. "He painted over an entire project once, just an hour before a showing, even though I was a wreck about him ruining the beautiful painting he'd done. He just kept slapping oils on the canvas, explaining that an uncommon life demanded an uncommon approach, and that he had all-new inspiration for his work."

The shared reminiscence brought Zach to life in full color for a moment, an experience Miles hadn't had in a long time. The action—and the words—were so completely in keeping with how he remembered his friend.

"He was a bright light," Miles agreed, remembering how often they'd looked up to his fearlessness and, later, stood beside him whenever he got into scrapes with schoolmates who weren't ready for the Zach Eldridges of the world.

"I never met anyone like him," Chiara continued, turning her mug in a slow circle on the table. "Not before, and not since." Halting the distracted movement, she took a sip from her cup before continuing. "I knew him well enough to have a crush on him, to the point that I thought I loved him. And maybe I did. Youthful romances can have a profound impact on us."

Miles searched her face, wondering if Chiara

had been aware of Zach's sexual orientation; he'd come out to his friends the summer before sophomore year. Had that been why things hadn't worked out between them?

But another thought quickly crowded that one out. A long-buried memory from the aftermath of that dark time in Miles's life.

"There was a girl who came to Dowdon after Zach's death. Around Christmastime." He remembered her telling Miles the same story. She loved Zach and needed the truth about what had happened to him. But Miles had been in the depths of his own grief, shell-shocked and still in denial about the cliff-jumping accident that had killed his friend.

Chiara studied him now, the long pause drawing his awareness to a clock ticking somewhere in the house.

"So you remember me?" she asked, her words jarring him.

He looked at her face more closely as slow recognition dawned. He couldn't have stopped the soft oath he breathed before he spoke again.

"That was you?"

Chiara watched the subtle play of emotions over Miles's face before he reined them in, regretting the way she'd handled things even more than when she'd first awoken.

But she couldn't back down on her mission. She would have answers about Zach's death.

"Yes." Her stomach clenched at the memory of sneaking onto the Dowdon campus that winter to question Zach's friends. "I spoke to you and to Gage Striker fourteen years ago, but both of you were clearly upset. Gage was openly hostile. You seemed...detached."

"That girl couldn't have been you." Miles's jaw flexed, his broad shoulders tensing as he straightened in his chair. "I would have remembered the name."

Defensiveness flared at the hard look in his blue eyes.

"I was born Kara Marsh, but it was too common for Instagram, so I made up Chiara Campagna when I launched my career." Perhaps it made her sound like she'd hidden something from him, but her brand had taken off years ago, and she no longer thought of herself as Kara. Her family certainly hadn't cared, taking more of an interest in her now that she was famous with a big bank account than they ever had when she was under their roof saving her babysitting money to pay for her own clothes. "I use the name everywhere for consistency's sake. While I don't try to conceal my identity, I also don't promote it."

"Yet you kissed me. Spent the night."

Her gaze lingered on the black Henley he was wearing with a pair of dark brown cargo pants, the fitted shirt calling to mind the feel of his body under her hands.

"That wasn't supposed to happen," she admitted, guilt pinching harder at the accusation in his voice.

"What took place between us was completely un-expected."

The defense sounded weak even to her ears. But he'd been there. He had to know how the passion had come out of nowhere, a force of nature.

The furrow in his brow deepened. "So you'll admit you were in my study last night, looking up Zach's name on my computer."

A chill crept through her. "You knew?" She bristled at the realization. "Yet you kissed me. Invited me to spend the night."

She parroted his words, reminding him he'd played a role in their charged encounter.

"You didn't clear the search history. A page of files with Zach's name on them was still open." He didn't address the fact that he'd slept with her anyway.

Because it hadn't mattered to him? Because *she* didn't matter? She stuffed down the hurt she had no business feeling, shoving aside the memories of how good things had been between them. She'd known even then that it couldn't last. She'd told herself as much when Miles had wrested a promise from her that he could have a date afterward. He wouldn't hold her to that now.

Steeling herself, she returned to her agenda. Her real priority.

"Then you know I'm desperate for answers." Regret burned right through all the steeliness. "I'm sorry I invaded your privacy. That was a mistake.

But I've been digging for clues about Zach's death for fourteen years. Now that the media spotlight has turned to the Mesa Falls owners thanks to your connection to Alonzo Salazar, I saw a chance to finally learn the truth."

"By using your invitation into my home to spy on me," he clarified.

"Why wasn't Zach's death in the papers? Why didn't the school acknowledge it?" She'd searched for years. His death notice had been a line item weeks after the fact, with nothing about the person he'd been or how he'd died.

"You say you were friends with him, but I only have your word on that." Miles watched her suspiciously. Judging her? She wondered what had happened to the man she'd been with the night before. The lover who'd been so generous. This cold stranger bore him no resemblance. "How do I know this isn't another attempt by the media to unearth a story?"

"Who else even knows about him but me?" she asked, affronted. Indignant. "There was never a public outcry about his death. No demand for answers from the media. Maybe because he was just some foster kid that—"

Her throat was suddenly burning and so were her eyes, the old emotions coming back to surprise her with their force while Miles studied her from across the breakfast table. With an effort, she regained control of herself and backed her chair away from the table.

"I'd better go," she murmured, embarrassed for the ill-timed display of feelings. But damn it, Zach had deserved a better send-off. She'd never even known where to attend a service for him, because as far as she'd known, there hadn't been one.

That broke her heart.

Miles rose with her, covering her hand briefly with his.

"It was a simple question. I meant no offense." He shifted his hand away, but the warmth remained where his fingers had been. "We've safeguarded our friend's memory for a long time, and I won't relax my protection of him now. Not for anyone."

She tilted her chin at him, trying her damnedest to see some hint of warmth in that chilly facade.

"What memory?" she pressed. "He vanished without a trace. Without an opportunity for his friends to mourn him."

"His friends *did* mourn him. They still do." His expression was fierce. "We won't allow his name to be drawn into the public spectacle that Alonzo Salazar brought to the ranch because of that damned tell-all book."

"I would never do that to Zach." She hugged her arms around herself, recalling too late that she wore Miles's clothes. Her fingers rested on the cotton of his sweats. The scent of him. As if she wasn't feeling vulnerable already. "As for his friends mourning him, you weren't the only ones. There were a lot of other people who cared about Zach. People who never got to say goodbye."

For a long minute, they regarded each other warily in the quiet room, the scents of their forgotten breakfast still savory even though no food could possibly tempt her. Her stomach was in knots.

But even now, in the aftermath of the unhappy exchange, awareness of him lingered. Warmth prickled along her skin as they stood facing each other in silent challenge, reminding her of the heat that had propelled her into his arms the night before.

The chime of her cell phone intruded on the charged moment, a welcome distraction from whatever it was that kept pulling her toward a man who was determined to keep his secrets. He was as quick to seize on the reprieve from their exchange as she was. He turned toward the table to begin clearing away their half-finished meal.

She retrieved the device from where it lay on the table, checking the text while she carried her coffee cup to the sink. The message was from her assistant, Jules.

All your platforms hacked. On phone with IG now. Sent help notices to the rest. Some joker who didn't like a post? I'm on it, but knew you'd want heads-up.

She didn't realize she'd gone still until she heard Miles asking, "What's wrong?"

Her brain couldn't quite compute what was wrong.

The timing of the attack on all her platforms at once seemed strange. Suddenly feeling a little shaky, she dropped into the closest seat, a bar stool at the island.

"Someone hijacked my social media accounts," she whispered, stunned and not buying that it was the work of a disgruntled commenter. "All of the platforms at once, which seems really unusual."

"Does that happen often?" Miles jammed the food in the huge refrigerator, working quickly to clean up.

"It's never happened before." She gulped back a sick feeling, tapping the tab for Instagram on her phone to see for herself. "I have friends who have had one platform hijacked here or there, but not all at once."

Miles dumped the remaining dishes in the sink and toweled off his hands before tossing the dishcloth aside. He rejoined her, gripping the back of her chair. "That feels like someone has an ax to grind."

The warmth of his nearness was a distraction she couldn't afford. She scooted forward in her seat.

"Someone with enough tech savvy to take over all my properties at once." She checked one profile after another, finding the photos changed, but still of her.

Less flattering images. Older images. But they weren't anything to be embarrassed about. She'd had friends whose profiles were hacked and replaced with digitally altered pictures that were highly compromising.

"Any idea who'd do something like that?" Miles asked, the concern in his voice replacing some of the animosity that had been there before. "Any enemies?"

"I can't think of anyone." She'd had her fair share of trolls on her account, but they tended to stir up trouble with other commenters as opposed to targeting her.

Her phone chimed again. She swiped the screen in a hurry, hopeful Jules had resolved the problem. But the text in her inbox was from a private number. Maybe one of the social media platforms' customer service used that kind of anonymous messaging?

She clicked open the text.

Today's takeover is a warning. Stay out of Zach's business or your accounts will be seriously compromised.

Her grip on the phone tightened. She blinked twice as the threat chilled her inside and out.

"Are you okay?" Miles touched her shoulder, the warmth of his fingers anchoring her as fear trickled through her.

"I've got to go." Shaky with the newfound realization that someone was keeping close tabs on her, she wondered who else could possibly know she was investigating Zach's death besides Miles.

She slid off the bar stool to her feet, needing to get back to her laptop and her assistant to figure out the extent of her cybersecurity problem. This felt like someone was watching her. Or tracking her online activity.

"You're pale as the snow." Miles steadied her by the elbow when she wobbled unsteadily. "What's going on?"

She didn't want to share what she'd just read with him when he mistrusted her. When she mistrusted him. But his touch overrode everything else, anchoring her in spite of the hollow feeling inside.

"Look." She handed him her phone, unable to articulate all the facets of the new worries wriggling to life. "I just received this." Pausing until he'd had time to absorb the news, she continued, "Who else even knows about Zach, let alone what I came here for?"

His jaw flexed as he stared at the screen, stubble giving his face a texture she remembered well from when he'd kissed her during the night. She fisted her hands in the pockets of the sweatpants to keep herself from doing something foolish, like running an exploratory finger along his chin.

"I didn't think anyone else remembered him outside of my partners and me." He laid her phone on the kitchen island behind her. "As for who else knows why you came here, I can't answer that, as I only found out moments ago."

She hesitated. "You saw my attempt to check your computer last night. So you knew then that I had an interest. Did you share that information with anyone?"

A scowl darkened his expression.

"I texted Gage Striker about an hour into the party to ask how well he knew you, since I thought you'd been going through my files."

She shouldn't be surprised that Miles had as much reason to suspect her of hiding something as she'd had to suspect him. She'd recognized that they'd been circling one another warily the previous night before the heat between them burned everything else away. If anything, maybe it soothed her grated nerves just a little to know he hadn't been any more able to resist the temptation than she had.

"And Gage could have told any one of your other partners. They, in turn, could have confided in friends or significant others." Reaching back to the counter, she retrieved the cell and shoved it in the pocket of Miles's sweats. "So word could have spread to quite a few people by this morning."

"In theory," he acknowledged, though his voice held a begrudging tone. "But Gage didn't even put in an appearance at the party. So he wouldn't have been around anyone else to share the news, and I'm guessing he had something big going on in his personal life that kept him from attending."

"Maybe he needed to hire someone to hack all my accounts." She couldn't rule it out, despite Miles's scoff. Anger ramped up inside her along with a hint of mistrust. "But for now, I need to return to my hotel and do everything I can to protect my brand."

"Wait." He stepped in front of her. Not too close, but definitely in her path.

Her pulse quickened at his nearness. Her gaze dipped to the way the fitted shirt with the Rivera Ranch logo skimmed his broad shoulders and arms. Her mouth dried up.

Maybe he felt the same jolt that she did, because he looked away from her, spearing a hand through his hair.

"Let me drive you back," he told her finally. "Someone might be watching you. And until you know what you're dealing with, you should take extra precautions for your safety."

The thought of spending more time alone with this man was too tempting. Which was why she absolutely had to decline. Things were confused enough between them already.

"I'll be fine. My assistant will send a car and extra security." She withdrew her phone again—a good enough excuse to take her eyes off him—and sent the request. "I just need to get my dress and I'll be on my way."

Still Miles didn't move.

"Where are you staying?" he pressed. "You can't ghost me. You owe me a date."

"I think we both know that's not a good idea in light of how much things have gone awry between us." She couldn't believe he'd even brought it up. But perhaps he only wanted to use that time with her as a way to keep tabs on her while she sought the information he was determined to keep private.

"I still want to see you." He didn't explain why. "Where will you be?"

"I've been in a local hotel, but today I've got a flight to Tahoe to spend time with Astrid. I haven't seen her since she had the baby."

Jonah and Astrid had a house on the lake near a casino resort owned by Desmond Pierce, another Mesa Falls partner. Spending time with Astrid would be a way to keep an eye on two of the ranch owners while removing herself from the temptation that Miles presented just by being in the same town.

Even now, looking into Miles's blue eyes, she couldn't help recalling the ways he'd kissed and touched her. Made her fly apart in his arms.

For now, she needed to regroup. Protect her business until she figured out her next move in the search for answers about Zach.

"I don't suppose it's a coincidence that half of the Mesa Falls partners live around Tahoe," Miles observed drily. "Maybe I should go with you. No doubt we'll be convening soon to figure out who could be threatening you. Zach's legacy is important to us."

She shrugged, averting her eyes because she knew they'd betray her desire for him. "You can look into it your way. I'll keep looking into it mine. But I don't think it's a good idea for us to spend more time alone together after what happened last night."

Just talking about it sent a small, pleasurable shiver up her spine. She had to hold herself very still to hide it. The least movement from him and she would cave to temptation.

"I disagree. And if we both want answers, maybe we should be working together instead of apart." His voice gentled, taking on that low rasp that had slid right past her defenses last night. "You wouldn't have checked my computer files if you didn't think I had information that could help you. Why not go straight to the source?"

For a moment, the idea of spending another day with him—another night—rolled over her like a seductive wave. But then she forced herself to shake it off.

"If you wanted to share information with me, you could tell me now." She put it out there like a dare, knowing he wouldn't spill any secrets.

He and his friends had never revealed anything about Zach. Not then. And not now. Because Miles was silent. Watchful. Wary.

Her phone chimed again, and she didn't need to check it to know her ride was out front.

"In that case, I'd better be going." She turned on her heel. "Maybe I'll see you in Tahoe."

"Chiara." He called her name before she reached the stairs leading back to the bedroom suite.

Gripping the wood rail in a white-knuckled grip, she looked over her shoulder at him.

"Be careful. We don't know who you're dealing with, but it could be someone dangerous."

The reminder brought the anxiety from earlier

churning back. She tightened her hold on the rail to keep from swaying.

"I'll be careful," she conceded before stiffening her spine with resolve. "But I'm not backing down."

Five

Miles began making phone calls as soon as Chiara left. He poured himself a drink and paced circles around the indoor pool, leaving voice messages for Gage and Jonah. Then he tapped the contact button for Desmond Pierce, his friend who owned the casino resort on Lake Tahoe.

For fourteen years, the friends who'd been with Zach Eldridge when he died had kept the circumstances a secret. At first, they'd done so because they were in shock and grieving. Later, they'd remained silent to protect his memory, as a way to honor him in death even though they'd been unable to save him.

But if someone outside the six friends who owned Mesa Falls knew about Zach—about the circumstances that had pushed him over the edge that fateful day—then his secrets weren't safe any longer. They needed to figure out their next steps.

A voice on the other end of the phone pulled him from his thoughts, and he paused his pacing around the pool to listen.

"Hey, Miles," Desmond answered smoothly, the slot machine chirps and muted conversation of the casino floor sounding in the background. "What's up?"

"Problems." As succinctly as possible, he summarized the situation with Chiara and the threat against her if she kept looking for answers about Zach's death.

When Miles was done, Desmond let out a low whistle. The sounds of the casino in the background had faded, meaning he must have sought privacy for the conversation.

"Who else knows about Zach but us?" Desmond asked. "Moreover, who the hell would have known Chiara was asking questions within hours of her showing up at Mesa Falls?"

Miles stared out the glass walls around the enclosed pool, watching the snow fall as he let the question hang there for a moment. He was certain Desmond must have come to the same conclusion as him.

"You know it points to one of us," Miles answered, rattling the last of the ice in his drink. "I texted Gage last night when I thought she was snooping in my office."

He didn't want to think Gage would go to the length of hacking her accounts to protect their secrets, but every one of the partners had his own reasons for not wanting the truth to come to light. Gage, in particular, bore a weight of guilt because his influential politician father had kept the truth of the accident out of the media. Nigel Striker had made a substantial grant to the Dowdon School to ensure the incident was handled the way he chose.

Quietly. Without any reference to Zach's connection to the school. Which explained why Chiara hadn't been able to learn anything about it.

Desmond cleared his throat. "Gage could have shared that information with any one of us."

"I can't believe we're even discussing the possibility of a leak within our group." The idea made everything inside him protest. They'd spent fourteen years trying to protect the truth.

Who would go rogue now and break that trust?

"Just because we're discussing it doesn't prove anything," Desmond pointed out reasonably. "Chiara could have confided her intentions to someone else. Or someone could have tracked her searches online."

"Right. But we need to meet. And this time, no videoconferencing." He remembered the way the last couple of meetings had gone among the partners— once with only four of them showing up in person, and another time with half of them participating remotely. "We need all six of us in the same room."

"You really think it's one of us?" Desmond asked. Despite Desmond's normally controlled facade, Miles could hear the surprise in his friend's tone.

"I'm not sure. But if it's not, we can rule it out faster if we're together in the same room. If one of us is lying, we'll know." Miles might not have spent much time in person with his school friends in the last fourteen years, but their bond ran deep.

They'd all agreed to run the ranch together in the hope of honoring Zach's life. Zach had loved the outdoors and the Ventana Wilderness close to their school. He would have appreciated Mesa Falls's green ranching mission to protect the environment and help native species flourish.

"Do you need help coordinating it?" Desmond asked, the sounds of the casino again intruding from his end of the call.

"No. I think we should meet in Tahoe this time. But I wanted to warn you that Chiara is on her way there even now. She says she's going to see Astrid, but I have the feeling she'll be questioning Jonah, too. She might even show up at your office." Miles couldn't forget the look in her eyes when she'd said she wouldn't back down from her search for answers about Zach.

There'd been a gravity that hinted at the strong stuff she was made of. He understood that kind of commitment. He felt it for Rivera Ranch, the family property he'd inherited and would protect at any cost.

Of course, he felt that way about Zach and Mesa Falls, too. Unfortunately, their strong loyalties to the same person were bound to keep putting them at odds. Unless they worked together. The idea made him uneasy. But did he really have a choice?

The thought of seeing her again—even though she'd only walked out his door an hour ago—sent anticipation shooting through him. He'd never forget the night they'd shared.

"I'll keep an eye out for her," Desmond assured him. "Thanks for the heads-up."

Miles disconnected the call and pocketed his phone. He would hand off the task of scheduling the owners' meeting to his assistant, since coordinating times could be a logistical nightmare. But no matter how busy they were, this had to take priority.

Things were coming to a head for Mesa Falls. And Zach.

And no matter how much Miles didn't trust Chiara Campagna, he was worried for her safety with someone threatening her. Which would have been reason enough for him to fly to Tahoe at the first opportunity. But he also couldn't deny he wanted to see her again.

She'd promised him a date. And he would hold her to her word.

That night, in her rented villa overlooking Lake Tahoe, Chiara tucked her feet underneath her in the window seat as she opened her tablet. The nine-bedroom home and guesthouse were situated next door to Desmond Pierce's casino resort, assuring her easy access to him. The separate guesthouse allowed her to have her assistant and photo team members nearby while giving all of them enough space. Astrid and Jonah lived just a few miles away, and Chiara would see them as soon as she could. She'd already made plans to meet Astrid for a spin class in the morning.

This was the first moment she'd had to herself all day. First there'd been the morning with Miles, then the flight to Truckee and drive to Tahoe Vista, with most of the travel time spent on efforts to stabilize her social media platforms.

She should probably be researching cybersecurity experts to ensure her social media properties were more secure in the future, even though she'd gotten all of her platforms corrected by dinnertime. It only made good business sense to protect her online presence. But she'd spent so many years making the right decisions for her public image, relentlessly driving her empire to keep growing that she couldn't devote one more minute to work today. Didn't she deserve a few hours to herself now and then? To be a woman instead of a brand?

So instead of working, she thumbed the remote button to turn on the gas fireplace and dimmed the spotlights in the exposed trusswork of the cathedral ceiling. Settling back against the yellow cushions of the window seat, Chiara returned her attention to the tablet and found herself scrolling through a web search about Miles Rivera.

She'd like to think it was all part of her effort to find out more about Zach. Maybe if she could piece together clues from the lives of his friends during the year of Zach's death, she would find something she'd overlooked. But as she swiped through images of Miles at the historic Rivera Ranch property in the Red Clover Valley of the Sierra Nevada foothills, pausing on a few of him at galas in Mesa Falls and at the casino on Lake Tahoe, she realized she had ulterior motives. Even on the screen he took her breath away.

He looked as at home in his jeans and boots as he did in black tie, and not just because he was a supremely attractive man. There was a comfort in his own skin, a certainty of his place in the world that Chiara envied. She'd been born to privilege as the daughter of wealthy parents, but she'd always been keenly aware she didn't belong. Her mother had never known what to do with her; she'd been awkward and gangly until she grew into her looks. As a girl, she'd been antisocial, preferring books to people. She'd lacked charm and social graces, a failure that confirmed her mother's opinion of her as a hopeless child. So she'd been packed off to boarding school on the opposite coast, where she'd retreated into her art until she met Zach, her lone friend.

Then Zach died, and her parents lost their fortune.

Chiara transferred to public school and made even fewer friends there than she had at Brookfield. She fit in nowhere until she founded her fictional world online. Her Instagram account had started as a way to take photos of beautiful things. That other people liked her view of the world had shocked her, but eventually she'd come to see that she was good at being social on the other side of a keyboard. By the time she gained real traction and popularity, her awkwardness in person didn't matter anymore. Her followers liked her work, so they didn't care if she said very little at public events. Fans seemed to equate her reticence with the aloofness they expected in a star. But inside, Chiara felt like a fraud, wrestling with impostor syndrome that she'd somehow forged an extravagant, envied life she didn't really deserve.

Her finger hovered over an image of Miles with an arm slung around his friend Alec Jacobsen and another around Desmond Pierce. It was an old photo, similar to the one she'd seen in Miles's office at his house. She thought it was taken around the time the six friends had bought Mesa Falls. She'd known even before she'd restarted her search for answers that the men who'd bought the ranch had been Zach's closest friends at Dowdon. One of them knew something. Possibly all of them. What reason would they have to hide the circumstances of his death?

She'd contacted his foster home afterward, and years later, she'd visited the department of social services for information about Zach. The state hadn't been under any legal obligation to release details of his death other than to say it was accidental and that issues of neglect in foster care hadn't been a concern. She'd had no luck tracking down his birth parents. But Miles knew something, or else he wouldn't have been so emphatic about protecting Zach's privacy.

Staring into Miles's eyes in the photograph didn't yield any answers. Just twenty-four hours ago, she'd been convinced he was her enemy in her search. Sleeping with Miles had shown her a different side of him. And reminiscing with him about Zach for those few moments over breakfast had reinforced the idea that he'd shared a powerful bond with their shared friend. What reason did Miles have to push her away?

When she found herself tracing the angles of his face on the tablet screen, Chiara closed the page in a hurry. She couldn't afford the tenderness of feeling that had crept up on her with regard to Miles Rivera. It clouded her mission. Distorted her perspective when she needed to be clearheaded.

Tomorrow, she'd find a way to talk to Desmond Pierce. Then she'd see if Alec Jacobsen was in town. If she kept pushing, someone would divulge something. Even if they didn't mean to.

Turning her gaze to the moon rising over the lake through the window, she squinted, trying to see beyond her reflection in the glass. She needed to learn something before her anonymous blackmailer discovered she was still asking questions. Because while she was prepared to risk everything—the fame, the following, the income that came from it—to find out the truth of Zach's death, she couldn't help hoping Miles didn't have anything to do with it.

"Dig deep for the next hill!" The spin class instructor kept up her running stream of motivational commentary from a stationary bike at the center of the casino resort's fitness studio. "If you want the reward, you've got to put in the work!"

Chiara hated exercise class in general, and early-morning ones even more, but her friend Astrid had insisted the spin class was the best one her gym offered. So Chiara had pulled herself out of bed at the crack of dawn for the last two mornings. She'd dragged Jules with her, and Astrid met them there to work out in a room that looked more like a dance club than a gym. With neon and black lights, the atmosphere was high energy and the hip-hop music intense. Sweating out her restlessness wasn't fun, but it felt like a way to excise some of the intense emotions being with Miles had stirred up.

"I can't do another hill," Astrid huffed from the cycle to Chiara's right, her blond braid sliding over her shoulder as she turned to talk. A former model from Finland, Astrid had happily traded in her magazine covers for making organic baby food since becoming a mother shortly before Christmas. "You know I love Katja, but being pregnant left me with no muscle tone."

"I would have chosen the yoga class," Chiara managed as she gulped air, her hamstrings burning and her butt numb from the uncomfortable seat. "So I blame this hell on you."

"I would be *sleeping*." Jules leaned over her handlebars from the bike on Chiara's left, her pink tank top clinging to her sweaty shoulders. "So I blame both of you."

"Please,".Chiara scoffed, running a skeptical eye over Jules's toned legs. "You were a competitive volleyball player. I've seen you play for hours."

Chiara's family had lived next door to Jules's once upon a time, and the Santors were more like family to her than her own had ever been. When her business had taken off, she'd made it her mission to employ as many of the family members as she could, enjoying the pleasure of having people she genuinely liked close to her. Even now, back in Los Angeles, Jules's mom was in charge of Chiara's house.

"Spiking balls and attacking the net do not require this level of cardio," Jules grumbled, although she dutifully kicked up her speed at their instructor's shouted command to "go hard."

Chiara felt light-headed from the exercise, skipping breakfast, and the swirl of flashing lights as they pedaled.

"We owe ourselves lunch out at least, don't we?" Astrid pleaded, letting go of her handlebars long enough to take a drink from her water bottle. "Jonah got us a sitter tomorrow for the first time since I had Katja, so I've got a couple of hours free."

"This is the first time?" Chiara asked, smiling in spite of the sweat, the aches and the gasping for air.

Astrid had been nervous about being a mom before her daughter was born, but she'd been adorably committed to every aspect of parenting. Chiara couldn't help but compare her friend's efforts with her own mother's role in her life. Kristina Marsh had handed her daughter off to nannies whenever possible, which might not have been a problem if there'd been a good one in the mix. But she tended to hire the cheapest possible household help in order to add to her budget for things like clothes and jewelry.

"I hate leaving her with anyone but Jonah," Astrid admitted, slowing her pedaling in spite of their coach's motivational exhortation to "grind it out."

"But I think it's important to have someone trained in Katja's routine in case something comes up and I need help in a hurry."

"Definitely." Chiara wasn't about to let her friend hover around the babysitter when she could get her out of the house for a little while. "Plus you deserve a break. It's been two months."

"That's what Jonah says." Astrid's soft smile at the thought of her husband gave Chiara an unexpected pang in her chest.

She hadn't realized until that moment how much she envied Astrid's rock-solid relationship with a man she loved and trusted. Chiara hadn't even given a second thought to her single status in years, content to pursue her work instead of romance when she had difficulty trusting people anyhow. And for good reason. Her family was so good at keeping secrets from her she hadn't known they'd lost everything until the headmistress at Brookfield told her they were sending her home because her tuition hadn't been paid in months.

Chiara shoved that thought from her head along with any romance envy. She cheered along with the rest of the class as the instructor blew her whistle to signal the session's end. Jules slumped over her handlebars as she recovered, clicking through the diagnostics to check her stats.

Chiara closed her eyes for a long moment to rest them from the blinking red and green lights. And, no surprise, an image of Miles Rivera appeared on the backs of her eyelids, tantalizing her with memories of their night together.

She could live to be a hundred and still not be able to account for how fast she'd ended up in his bed. The draw between them was like nothing she'd ever experienced.

Astrid's softly accented words broke into Chiara's sensual reverie.

"So where should we meet for lunch tomorrow?" The hint of Finland in Astrid's words folded "where" to sound like "vere," the lilt as attractive as every other thing about her. "Des's casino has a bunch of places."

Chiara's eyes shot open at the mention of Desmond Pierce, one of Miles's partners. She needed to question him and Astrid's husband, Jonah, too. Subtly. And, ideally, close to the same time so neither one had a chance to warn the others about Chiara's interest in the details of Zach's final days.

"The casino is perfect." Chiara slid off her cycle and picked up her towel and water bottle off the floor, locking eyes with another woman who lingered near the cycles—a pretty redhead with freckles she hadn't noticed earlier. Why did she look vaguely familiar? Distracted, she told Astrid, "Pick your favorite place and we'll meet there."

The redhead scurried away, and Chiara guessed she didn't know the woman after all.

"There's an Indo-Mexican fusion spot called Spice Pavilion. I'm addicted to the tikka tacos." Astrid checked her phone as the regular house lights came up and the spin class attendees shuffled out of the room. "Can you do one o'clock? Jonah has a meeting that starts at noon, so I can shop first and then meet you."

A meeting? Chiara's brain chased the possibilities of what that might mean while she followed Jules toward the locker room, with Astrid behind them.

"Perfect," Chiara assured her friend as they reached the lockers and retrieved their bags. "Is Jonah's meeting at the casino, too?"

"Yes. More Mesa Falls business," Astrid answered as she hefted her quilted designer bag onto one shoulder and shut the locker with her knee. "Things have been heating up for the ranch ever since that tell-all book came out."

Didn't she know it. Chiara had plenty of questions of her own about the ranch and its owners, but she'd tried not to involve Astrid in her hunt for answers since she wouldn't use a valued friendship for leverage.

But knowing that Zach's friends would be congregating at the resort tomorrow was welcome information.

"Then you can leave Jonah to his meeting and we'll gorge ourselves on tikka tacos," Chiara promised her, calling the details over her shoulder to Jules, who had a locker on the next row. "Today I'm going to finish my posts for the week, so I can clear the whole day tomorrow. Text me if you're done shopping early or if you want company."

If all the men of Mesa Falls were in town, there was a chance she'd run into one of them at the casino anyhow. Desmond Pierce had been avoiding her calls, so she hadn't even gotten a chance to meet him. But she needed to speak to all of them.

Although there was one in particular she couldn't wait to see, even though she already knew he had nothing else to say to her on the subject of Zach's death.

Miles might be keeping secrets from her. And he might be the last man she'd ever trust with her heart because of that. But that didn't mean that she'd stopped thinking about his hands, his mouth or his body on hers for more than a few seconds at a time since she'd left Montana.

No doubt about it—she was in deep with this man, and they'd only just met.

Six

Steering his borrowed SUV around a hairpin turn, Miles pulled up to the massive lakefront villa where Chiara was staying for the week. He'd been in town for all of a few hours before seeking her out, but ever since he'd heard from Jonah that the place she'd rented was close to the casino where Miles was staying, he'd needed to see her for himself.

The property was brightly lit even though the sun had just set, the stone turrets and walkways illuminated to highlight the architectural details. Huge pine trees flanked the building, while a second stone guesthouse sat at an angle to the villa with a path linking them.

Stepping out of the casino's Land Rover that he'd

commissioned for the evening, Miles hoped all the lights meant that Chiara was taking her security seriously. He'd kept an eye on her social media sites since she'd left Mesa Falls to make sure no one hacked them again, but that hadn't done nearly enough to soothe his anxiety where she was concerned. Someone was threatening her for reasons related to Zach, and that did not sit well with him. He'd messaged her earlier in the day to let her know he would be in town tonight, but she hadn't replied.

Now, walking up the stone path into the central turret that housed the front entrance, he tucked his chin into the collar of his leather jacket against the chill in the wind. He could see into one of the large windows. A fire burned in the stone hearth of a great room, but he didn't notice any movement inside.

He shot a text to Chiara to warn her he was outside, then rang the bell. No sense adding to her unease during a week that had already upset her.

An instant later, he heard a digital chime and the bolt sliding open, then the door swung wide. Chiara stood on the threshold, her long dark hair held off her face with a white cable-knit headband. She wore flannel pajama bottoms in pink-and-white plaid. A V-neck cashmere sweater grazed her hips, the pink hue matching her fuzzy socks.

She looked sweetly delicious, in fact. But his overriding thought was that she shouldn't be answering her own door while someone was watching her movements and threatening her. Fear for her safety made him brusque.

"What happened to taking extra precautions with your safety?" He didn't see anyone else in the house with her. No bodyguard. No assistant.

Tension banded his chest.

"Hello to you, too." She arched a brow at him. "And to answer your question, the door was locked, and the alarm system was activated." She stepped to one side, silently inviting him in. "I gave my head of security the evening off since I had no plans to go out."

Relieved she'd at least thought about her safety, he entered the foyer, which opened into the great room with its incredible views of the lake. He took in the vaulted ceilings and dark wood accents along the pale walls. The scent of popcorn wafted from deeper in the house, the sound of popping ongoing.

"Right. I realize the level of security you use is your own business, I've just been concerned." He noticed a throw blanket on the floor in front of the leather sofa. A nest of pillows had been piled by the fireplace, and there was a glass of red wine on the hearth. "Early night?"

"My job isn't always a party every evening, contrary to popular opinion." She hurried toward the kitchen, a huge light-filled space separated from the great room by a marble-topped island. "Have a seat. I don't want my popcorn to burn."

He followed more slowly, taking in the honey-colored floors and pale cabinets, the row of pendant lamps casting a golden glow over the island counter, where a popcorn popper quickly filled with fluffy white kernels. The excessive size and grandeur of the space reminded him they moved in very different circles. For all of his wealth, Miles spent most of his time on his ranch. His life was quiet. Solitary. Hers was public. Extravagant.

But at least for now, they were alone.

"I didn't mean to intrude on your evening." He had to admit she looked at home in her sprawling rented villa, her down-to-earth pj's and sweater a far cry from the metallic dress she'd worn to the ranch party. She seemed more approachable. "I'm in town to meet with my partners, and I wanted to make sure there have been no new incidents."

He lowered himself onto a backless counter stool, gladder than he should be to see her again. She'd been in his thoughts often enough since their night together, and not just because he'd been concerned about her safety. Her kiss, her touch, the sound of her sighs of pleasure had distracted him day and night.

"Nothing since I left your house. Can I get you a glass of wine?" she asked, turning the bottle on the counter. "It's nothing special, but it's my preferred pairing with popcorn."

Her light tone hinted she wanted to change the subject from the threat she'd received, but he was unwilling to let it go.

"No, thank you. I won't keep you long." He stood

again, if only to get closer to her while she leaned a hip on the island.

The urge to pull her against him was so strong he forced himself to plant a palm on the marble countertop instead of reaching for her.

"Well, you don't need to fear for my safety. My assistant's boyfriend is also my bodyguard, and they're both staying in the guesthouse right on the property." She pointed out the window in the direction of the smaller lodge he'd seen close by. "I'm in good hands."

He'd prefer she was in *his* hands. But he ignored the need to touch her; he was just glad to hear she hadn't taken the threat lightly.

"Did you report the incident to the police?" His gaze tracked her emerald eyes before taking in her scrubbed-clean skin and high cheekbones. She smelled like orange blossoms.

"I didn't reach out to them." She frowned, folding her arms. "I was so busy that day trying to get all my social media accounts secured that I never gave it any thought."

He hated to upset her unnecessarily, but her safety was important to him. "You should let the authorities know you're being harassed. Even if they can't do anything to help, it would be good to have the episode on the record in case things escalate."

She mattered to him. Even when he knew that was problematic. She didn't trust him, and he had plenty of reason not to trust her. Yet that didn't stop him from wanting to see her again. He could tell himself all day it was because staying close to her would help him protect Zach's memory. But he wasn't that naive. The truth was far simpler. Their one night together wasn't nearly enough to satisfy his hunger for this woman.

"I'll report it tomorrow," she conceded with a nod, her dark hair shifting along her sweater. "I can head to the local station in the morning, before I have lunch with Astrid."

"Would you like me to go with you?" he offered, his hand leaving the marble counter to rest on top of hers. Briefly. Because if he touched her any longer, it would be damn near impossible to keep his head on straight. "Spending hours at the cop shop is no one's idea of fun."

A hint of a smile curved her lips. "I'll be fine," she insisted.

Refusing his offer, but not moving her fingers out from under his. He shifted fractionally closer.

Her head came up, her gaze wary. Still, he thought there might have been a flash of hot awareness in those beautiful eyes.

"What about the date you promised me?" He tipped up her chin to better see her face, read her expression.

She sucked in a quick breath. Then, as if to hide the reaction, she bit her lip.

He imagined the soft nip of those white teeth on his own flesh, a phantom touch.

"Name the day," he coaxed her as the moment drew out, the desire to taste her getting stronger with each passing breath.

"I told you that it's a bad idea for us to spend more time together," she said finally, not sounding the least bit sure of herself. "Considering how things spiraled out of control after the party at your house."

He skimmed a touch along her jaw, thinking about all the ways he hadn't touched her yet. All the ways he wanted to.

"I've spent so much time thinking about that night, I'm not sure I can regret it." His gaze dipped to the lush softness of her mouth. He trailed his thumb along the seam. "Can you?"

Her lips parted, a soft huff of her breath grazing his knuckle.

"Maybe not." She blinked fast. "But just because you successfully run into and escape from a burning building once doesn't mean you should keep tempting fate with return trips."

"Is that what this is?" He released her, knowing he needed to make his case with his words and not their combustible connection. "A burning building?"

"You know what I mean. We seem destined to be at odds while I search for answers about Zach. There's no point blurring the battle lines." She spoke quickly, as if eager to brush the whole notion aside so she could move on.

He hoped the hectic color in her cheeks was evidence that he affected her even a fraction of how much she tempted him. But he didn't want to press her more tonight for fear she'd run again. For now, he would have to content himself that she'd agreed to speak to the police tomorrow.

"Then we'll have to disagree on that point." He shoved his hands in the pockets of the leather jacket he'd never removed. "The fact is, you owe me a date, and I'm not letting you off the hook."

Still, he backed up a step, wanting to give her space to think it over.

"You're leaving?" She twisted a dark strand of hair around one finger.

He would not think about how that silky hair had felt wrapped around his hand the night they'd been together. "You deserve an evening to yourself. And while I hope you'll change your mind about a date, I'm not going to twist your arm. I have the feeling we'll run across each other again this week since we have a common interest in Zach's story."

"Maybe we will." Her bottle-green eyes slid over him before she squared her shoulders and picked up her bowl of popcorn. "Good night, Miles."

He would have liked to end the night very differently, but he would settle for her roaming gaze and the memory of her biting her lip when they touched. Those things might not keep him warm tonight, but they suggested the odds were good of her landing in his bed again.

For now, that was enough.

* * *

So much for her relaxing evening in front of the fire with popcorn and a book.

Chiara couldn't sit still after Miles left. Unsatisfied desires made her twitchy and restless. After half an hour of reading the same page over and over again in her book, never once making sense of it, she gave up. She replaced the throw blanket and pillows on the sofa, then took her wine and empty popcorn bowl into the kitchen.

Even now, as she opened her laptop and took a seat at the island countertop, she swore she could feel the place where Miles's thumb had grazed her lip. That, in turn, had her reliving his kisses and the way their bodies had sought one another's that night in Mesa Falls.

Could that kind of electrifying chemistry be wrong? She guessed *yes*, because she and Miles were going to be at odds over Zach. All the sizzling attraction in the world was only going to confuse her real goal—to honor Zach's memory by clearing away the mystery of his death.

But denying that she felt it in the first place, when she wasn't deceiving anyone with her protests, seemed foolish. Miles had surely recognized the attraction she felt for him. And yet he'd walked away tonight, letting her make the next move.

Instead of losing herself in his arms, she opted to search her files on Zach one more time. Checking her inbox, she noticed a retired administrator from

Dowdon School had gotten back to her on an email inquiry she'd made long ago. Or, more accurately, the administrator's former assistant had responded to Chiara. She hadn't asked directly about Zach; instead, she'd asked for information about the school year when he'd died under the guise of writing a general retrospective for a class reunion.

Apparently, the assistant hadn't cared that she wasn't a former student. She had simply attached a few files, including some flyers for events around campus, including one for the art fair where Chiara had last seen Zach. There was also a digital version of the small Dowdon yearbook.

After saving all the files, she opened them one by one. The art fair poster brought a sad, nostalgic smile to her face but yielded no clues. Seeing it reminded her how much of an influence Zach had on her life, though, his eye for artistic composition inspiring her long afterward. Other pamphlets advertised an author visit, a homecoming dance in conjunction with Brookfield and a football game. She wrote down the email contact information for the dance and sent a message to the address, using the same pretext as before.

Pausing to sip her wine, Chiara swiped through the yearbook even though she'd seen it twice before. Once, as soon as it came out; she'd made an excuse to visit the Brookfield library to examine a copy since the school kept all the Dowdon yearbooks in a special collection. She only paged through it enough to know Zach hadn't been in there. No photo. No mention.

Like he'd never existed.

Then, a year ago, she'd seen Jonah's copy at Astrid's house and had flipped through. Now, she examined the content more carefully in the hope of finding anything she'd overlooked.

First, however, she searched for Miles's photo. He was there, alphabetized in his class year next to his brother, Weston Rivera. They weren't twins, but they were as close in age as nontwin siblings could be.

The Rivera men had been swoonworthy even then. Wes's hair had been longer and unruly, his hazel eyes mischievous, and his look more surfer than rancher. Miles appeared little changed since the photo was taken, beyond the obvious maturing of his face and the filling out of the very male body she remembered from their night together. But his serious aspect and set jaw were the same even then, his blue eyes hinting at the old soul inside.

Before she could stop herself, her finger ran over his image on the screen.

Catching herself in the midst of fanciful thinking, she dismissed the unfamiliar romantic notions that had somehow attached themselves to Miles. She navigated away from the student photos section to browse the rest of the yearbook while she nibbled a few pieces of cold popcorn.

Half an hour later, a figure caught her eye in the background of one of the candid group shots taken outdoors on the Dowdon soccer field. It was a young woman in a knee-length navy blue skirt and sensible flats, her blond hair in a side part and low ponytail.

An old memory bubbled to the surface of seeing the woman. And she was a woman, not a girl, among the students, looking more mature than those around her.

Chiara had seen her before. Just once. Long ago. With Zach.

The thrill of discovery buoyed her, sending her mind twirling in twenty directions about what to do with the new information. Funny that the first person who came to mind to share it with was Miles.

Would he know the woman? She picked up her phone, seeing his contact information still on the screen since the last message she'd received had been from him, letting her know he was at her door. The desire to share this with him was strong. Or was it only her desire to see him again? The ache of seeing him walk out her door was still fresh.

With an effort, she set the phone aside.

As much as she wanted to see if Miles recognized the mystery woman, she acknowledged that he might not answer her truthfully. He'd made it clear he planned to keep Zach's secrets. That she couldn't trust someone who could turn her inside out with a look was unsettling.

Tonight, she would research all she could on her own. Tomorrow, she would meet Astrid for lunch and—with a little good luck in the timing department—maybe she could waylay Astrid's husband before he went into his meeting with the Mesa Falls partners.

All she wanted was a real, unfiltered reaction to the image of the woman she'd seen with Zach. Miles was too guarded, and he knew her motives too well. Perhaps Jonah wouldn't be as careful.

Intercepting one of the Mesa Falls partners before the meeting Astrid had mentioned proved challenging. Chiara arrived at the Excelsior early, but with multiple parking areas and valet service, the casino resort didn't have a central location where she could monitor everyone who entered the building. For that matter, having her bodyguard with her made it difficult to blend in, so she'd asked Stefan to remain well behind her while she scoped out the scene.

Chiara decided to surveil the floor with the prominent high-roller suite the group had used for a meeting a month ago when she had first started keeping tabs on them. She hurried up the escalator near a courtyard fountain among the high-end shops. Water bubbled and splashed from the mouth of a sea dragon into a marble pool at the base of the fountain, the sound a soothing murmur when her nerves were wound tight. The resort was already busy with tourists window-shopping and taking photos.

As she reached the second-floor gallery, she spotted Gage Striker entering the suite. The huge, tattooed New Zealander was too far ahead for her to flag his attention, but at least she knew she was in the right place. Maybe Jonah and Astrid would come this way soon. As she darted around a pair of older ladies wearing matching red hats, Chiara pulled her phone from her handbag shaped like a rose, wanting the device ready with the right screen to show Jonah the photo of the mystery woman.

A voice from over her right shoulder startled her.

"Looking for someone?"

The deep rasp that could only belong to Miles skittered along her nerve endings.

Her body responded instantly, thrilled at the prospect of this man's nearness. But she battled back those feelings to turn toward him coolly.

"You're not much for traditional greetings, are you?" She eyed his perfectly tailored blue suit, the jacket unbuttoned over a subtly pinstriped gray shirt with the collar undone. Her attention snagged on the hint of skin visible at the base of his neck before she remembered what she was saying. "Most people open with something like *hello*. Or *nice to see you, Chiara*."

A hint of a smile lifted his lips on one side as he stopped just inches from her. With any other man getting this close, Stefan might have come to her side, but her security guard had been at the party in Mesa Falls the night Chiara stayed with Miles. Stefan didn't intervene now.

"Maybe other people can't appreciate the pleasure

I find in catching you off guard." Miles lingered on the word *pleasure*.

Or else she did. She couldn't be certain. She was too distracted by the hint of his aftershave hovering between them.

"I'm joining Astrid for lunch while Jonah attends another super-secret Mesa Falls meeting." She glanced at her nails and pretended to inspect her manicure. She'd far rather he think her superficial than affected by his nearness.

Miles studied her. Keeping her focus on her hands, she felt his gaze more than saw it. She wouldn't have a chance to speak to Jonah now. Not without Miles being present, anyway. While she considered her plan B, a group of women in tiaras and feather boas strolled past, with the one in the center wearing a pink sash that said, "Birthday Girl."

"How did it go at the police station?" Miles asked, his fingers alighting on her forearm to draw her farther from the thoroughfare that led to the second-floor shops.

There were two couches in front of the high-roller suite and a low, clear cocktail table between them. Miles guided her to the area between the couches and the door to the suite, affording them a little more privacy.

"I had some other things to take care of this morning, but I'll call after lunch." She'd been so consumed with finding out the identity of the woman in the yearbook photo, she'd forgotten all about reporting the harassment.

Miles frowned. "I can't in good conscience let you put it off. After the meeting, I'll take you myself."

She bristled at his air of command. "I don't need an escort. I'll take care of it."

He pressed his lips together, as if reining in his emotions for a moment before he spoke. "Remember when you told me you had to be a one-woman content creator, marketing manager and finance director?" He clearly recalled how she'd defended her hard work when he'd been dismissive of her job. "Why don't you let someone else give you a hand?"

His thoughtfulness, underscored by how well he'd listened to her, made her relax a little. "It does sound better when you say it like that," she admitted.

"Good. And this way, you can ask me all the questions you want about the meeting." He nodded as if the matter was settled.

"Any chance you'll actually answer them?" She wasn't sure it was wise for them to spend more time alone together, but maybe she could find a way to ask him about the photo of the unidentified woman without putting his guard up.

"I've said all along we should be working together." He took her hand in his, holding it between them while he stroked her palm with his thumb. "Where should I look for you after I finish up here?"

Her breath caught from just that smallest of touches. Her heart pounded harder.

"Spice Pavilion," she answered, seeing Astrid and Jonah heading toward them out of the corner of her eye.

"I'll look forward to it." Miles lifted the back of her hand to his lips and kissed it before releasing her.

Skin tingling pleasantly, she watched him disappear into the high-roller suite and wondered what she'd just gotten herself into. She noticed his brother followed him a moment later, while Astrid and Jonah gave each other a lingering goodbye kiss nearby. The blatant public display of affection seemed all the more romantic considering the couple were new parents.

What would it be like to have that kind of closeness with someone day in and day out?

Not that she would be finding out. Although her recent night with Miles reminded her how rewarding it was to share passion, she owed it to Zach not to let the connection distract her from her goal. She would spend time with Miles because he was still her most promising resource for information. And despite the coincidental timing of the threats against her, she'd had time to realize Miles was too honorable a man to resort to those tactics. She was safe with him.

She just had to find a way to get him talking.

Seven

Restless as hell, Miles prowled the perimeter of the high-roller suite, waiting for the meeting to get underway. Weston and Desmond were deep in conversation on a curved leather sofa in the center of the room, while a server passed through the living area with a tray of top-shelf bottles. Gage stared down into the fire burning in a sleek, modern hearth, a glass of his preferred bourbon already in hand. A massive flat-screen television was mounted over the fireplace, but the display was dark. In the past, the group had used the screens to teleconference in the missing Mesa Falls owners, but today all were present in person. Even Jonah, the new father, and Alec Jacobsen, the game developer who spent most of his time globe-hopping to get inspiration for the complex world-building required for his games. The two of them lounged near the pool table.

On either side of the fireplace, windows overlooked Lake Tahoe, the clear sky making the water look impossibly blue. Miles paused by one of them, waving off the offer of a beverage from the bow-tied server. He'd need his wits sharp for his meeting with Chiara afterward.

Hell, maybe he needed to worry more about having his instincts honed for the meeting with his friends. The possibility of a traitor to their shared cause had kept him up at night ever since Chiara had been threatened. He'd never doubted the men in this room before. But who else even knew about Zach to make a threat like the one Chiara had received?

"Are we ready?" Miles stopped pacing to ask the question, his back to a mahogany bookcase. He wasn't usually the one to spearhead discussions like this, but today the need for answers burned hot. "I know you're all busy. The sooner we figure out a plan, the sooner we can all go home."

Desmond gave a nod to the server, who left the room quickly, closing the door to the multilevel suite behind her. As the owner of Excelsior, Desmond commanded the operations of the resort and served as their host when they met on the property.

Weston cleared his throat. "Can you bring us up to speed on what's happening?"

The fact that his brother was the first to respond to

him surprised Miles given the enmity between him and Wes that had started when they'd been pitted against one another at an early age by their parents. The tension had escalated years ago when they'd briefly dated the same woman. But they'd made strides to put that behind them over the last year. Miles suspected Wes had mellowed since finding love with April Stephens, the financial investigator who'd discovered where the profits of Alonzo's book were going.

"Chiara Campagna has been digging around to find out how Zach died. She knew him in school," he told them bluntly, fisting his hands in the pockets of his pants as he tried to gauge the reactions of his friends. "She attended Brookfield before she became an internet sensation, and she met Zach through the school's art program."

There were no murmurs of reaction. The only sound in the room was the clink of ice cubes in a glass as a drink shifted. But then, they'd known the meeting was called to discuss this issue before walking in the door. So Miles continued.

"She wants to know the circumstances of Zach's death, suspecting some kind of cover-up since there was no news released about it." As he explained it, he understood her frustration. And yes, pain.

Just because she'd been a fifteen-year-old with a crush on a friend didn't diminish their connection.

He recognized the power and influence those early relationships could hold over someone.

Near the fireplace, Gage swore and finished his drink. His influential father had been the one to insist the story of Zach's accident remain private. The gag order surrounding the trauma had been one more complication in an already thorny situation.

"But why now?" Alec asked, spinning a cue ball like a top under one finger while he slouched against the billiard table. He wore a T-shirt printed with shaded outlines of his most iconic game characters, layered under a custom suit jacket. "Zach's been dead for fourteen years. Doesn't it seem strange that she's taken a renewed interest now?"

"No." Gage stalked over to the tray the server had left on the glass-topped cocktail table and helped himself to another shot of bourbon, tattoos flashing from the cuffs of his shirtsleeves as he poured the drink. "Chiara told Elena that she'd given up searching for answers about Zach until the Alonzo Salazar story broke at Christmas. With Mesa Falls and all of us in the spotlight, Chiara saw an opportunity to press harder for the truth."

Miles mulled over the new information about Chiara, interested in anything he could gather about the woman who dominated his thoughts. Elena Rollins was a lifestyle blogger who'd visited Mesa Falls to chase a story on Alonzo, but she'd ended up falling for Gage and had backed off. The two women had developed a friendship when Chiara had lent the power of her social media platform to bolster Elena's following.

"But that opportunity is going away now that we've given the public a story about where the profits from Alonzo's book went," Alec chimed in again, using his fingers to shoot the eight ball into a side pocket with a backspin. "Media interest will die out, and we'll go back to living in peace. No one needs to find out anything about Zach."

Even now, it was difficult to talk about the weekend that Zachary Eldridge had jumped to his death off a cliff into the Arroyo Seco River. The men in this room had once argued to the point of violence over whether Zach had planned to take his own life or it had truly been an accident. Eventually, they'd agreed to disagree about that, but they'd made a pact to keep their friend's memory away from public speculation. It had been tough enough for them to deal with the possibility that Zach had jumped to his death on purpose. The thought of dredging all that up again was...unbearable.

"Maybe. Maybe not," Miles returned slowly, turning it over in his head, trying to see what they knew from another angle. "But just because the public doesn't know about the mystery benefactor of the book profits doesn't mean we should just forget about him. We know the boy is thirteen years old puts his conception around the time of the accident. The last time we met, we were going to have a detective track the boy and his guardian."

He didn't remind them of the rest of what they needed to know—if there was a chance any of them had fathered the child.

Around the holidays, a woman had worked briefly at the ranch under the alias Nicole Smith and had claimed that Alonzo's book profits were supporting her dead sister's son—a boy born in a hospital close to Dowdon School seven and a half months after Zach's death. But before any of the ranch owners could speak to her directly, Nicole was abruptly fired. When they'd tried to track down the supervisor responsible for dismissing her, they learned the guy had quit the next day and didn't leave a forwarding address.

All of which raised uncomfortable questions about the integrity of the group in this room. Had one of them ordered the woman's dismissal? Had Nicole been too close to the truth—that Alonzo Salazar had been helping to support Nicole's nephew because he knew who'd fathered the boy? They'd learned that the woman's real name was Nicole Cruz, and they'd obtained some basic information about the boy, Matthew. But they were trying to find her to meet with her in person.

"I'm handling that." Weston sat forward on the couch to flick on the huge wall-mounted television screen controlled by a tablet in front of him. "A detective is following a lead to Nicole and Matthew Cruz in Prince Edward Island. He's supposed to land tonight to check out the address."

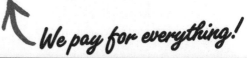

Complete the survey below and return
it today to receive up to **4 FREE BOOKS**
and **FREE GIFTS** guaranteed!

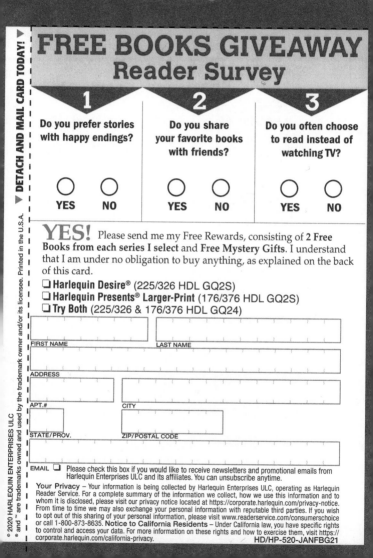

▼ DETACH AND MAIL CARD TODAY! ▼

Printed in the U.S.A.

© 2020 HARLEQUIN ENTERPRISES ULC
® and ™ are trademarks owned and used by the trademark owner and/or its licensee.

FREE BOOKS GIVEAWAY
Reader Survey

1
Do you prefer stories
with happy endings?

○ YES   ○ NO

2
Do you share
your favorite books
with friends?

○ YES   ○ NO

3
Do you often choose
to read instead of
watching TV?

○ YES   ○ NO

YES! Please send me my Free Rewards, consisting of **2 Free
Books from each series I select** and **Free Mystery Gifts.** I understand
that I am under no obligation to buy anything, as explained on the back
of this card.

❏ Harlequin Desire® (225/326 HDL GQ2S)
❏ Harlequin Presents® Larger-Print (176/376 HDL GQ2S)
❏ Try Both (225/326 & 176/376 HDL GQ24)

FIRST NAME   LAST NAME

ADDRESS

APT.#   CITY

STATE/PROV.   ZIP/POSTAL CODE

EMAIL ❏ Please check this box if you would like to receive newsletters and promotional emails from
Harlequin Enterprises ULC and its affiliates. You can unsubscribe anytime.

HD/HP-520-JANFBG21

HARLEQUIN READER SERVICE—Here's how it works:

Wes flicked through a series of photos on his tablet that then appeared on the TV screen, images of Nicole and Matthew—neither of whom they recognized—followed by grainy security system footage from when Nicole had worked at the ranch, as well as some shots of the boy from his former school. The different angles didn't do anything to help Miles recognize the boy.

"With any luck, the detective finds them." Miles turned his attention back to his colleagues. "And brings them to Mesa Falls so we can speak to the guardian at length and request permission to run a DNA test on the boy."

"Right." Wes clicked to another slide labeled "instructions for obtaining DNA."

"In the meantime, I've sent you all the file and collection kits by courier service. Most of you have already submitted yours, but we still need samples from Gage and Jonah. I've got a shipper ready to take them before you leave the meeting today. Alonzo's sons have already provided samples."

The silence in the room was thick. Did Jonah or Gage have reasons for dragging their feet? It had taken Miles two seconds to put a hair in a vial and ship the thing out.

Jonah blew out a sigh as he shoved away from the pool table and wandered over to a piano in the far corner of the room. He plunked out a few chords while he spoke. "That's fine. But none of us is going to be the father. Alonzo would have never stood by idly and paid for the boy's education if any of us were the dad. He would have demanded we own up to our responsibility once we were old enough to assume that duty."

"Maybe he was a mentor to the boy's mother, and not the father," Gage mused aloud, not sounding convinced. "This kid might not have anything to do with us."

"Possibly," Wes agreed. "But the kid was important to Alonzo, and that makes him important to us. Let's rule out the more obvious connection first."

"Agreed." Miles met his brother's hazel eyes, trying to remember the last time they'd been on the same page about anything. "But the more pressing issue today is that Chiara's social media accounts were hacked and she received an anonymous text threatening more attacks if she kept pursuing answers about Zach's death."

Recalling that morning at his house, Miles felt anger return and redouble that someone had threatened her, a woman who'd gotten under his skin so fast he hasn't seen it coming. That it had happened while she was in his home, as his guest, only added to his sense of responsibility. That it could be one of his friends, or someone close to them, chilled him.

"Anyone remember her from when she attended Brookfield?" Gage asked as Wes switched the image on the screen to show a school yearbook photo of Chiara. "When she was known as Kara Marsh?"

Wariness mingled with suspicion as Miles swung around to face Gage. "You knew?"

He'd texted Gage that night to ask him what he knew about Chiara, and he'd never mentioned it.

"Not until two days ago." Gage held both hands up in a sign of his innocence. "Elena told me. She and Chiara have gotten close in the last month. Apparently Chiara mentioned she used to go by a different name and that none of us remembered her even though she attended a school near Dowdon. If she confided in Elena, she obviously wasn't trying to hide it. And Astrid must be aware."

Miles studied Gage's face but couldn't see any hint of falseness there. Of all of them, Gage was the most plainspoken and direct. The least guarded. So it was tough to envision the big, bluff New Zealander keeping secrets.

From across the room, Alec's voice sliced through his thoughts.

"I remember Kara Marsh." Alec's eyes were on the television screen. "She came to Dowdon that Christmas asking questions about Zach."

Of all the friends, Alec had been closest to Zach. After the accident, he had retreated the most. To the point that Miles had sometimes feared the guy would follow in Zach's footsteps. He'd wondered if they'd wake up one morning to find out Alec had stepped off a cliff's edge in the middle of the night. Alonzo Salazar had shared the concern, speaking privately to all of them about signs to look for when people contemplated suicide. Alec came through it, as they all had. They were good now. Solid. But it had been a rough year.

"Did you talk to her?" Miles asked, needing to learn everything he could about Chiara.

He'd called this meeting out of a need to protect Zach's memory. And yet he felt a need to protect Chiara, too. To find out if any of his partners were the source of the leak that led to Chiara's getting hacked. He'd been watching them all carefully, studying their faces, but he hadn't seen any hint of uneasiness in any one of them.

"No." Alec shook his head as he stroked his jaw, looking lost in thought before his gaze came up to fix on Miles. "But you did. She spoke to you, and then she went to Gage. I was hanging out under the bleachers near the football field with—" he hesitated, a small smile flashing before it disappeared again "—with a girl I knew. Anyway, I was there when I saw Kara sneak onto the campus through the back fence."

"You followed her?" Jonah asked, dropping onto the bench in front of the piano.

Alec shrugged, flicking a white cue ball away from him where he still leaned against the pool table. "I did. The girl I was with was in a snit about it, but I wanted to see what Kara was up to. Besides, in those days, I was more than happy to look for diversions wherever I could find them."

They had all been emotionally wrecked during

those weeks, not sleeping, barely eating, unable to even talk to each other since being together stirred up painful memories. Miles had thrown himself into work, taking a part-time job in the nearest town to get away from school as much as possible.

"Did Chiara see you?" Miles wished like hell he remembered that day more clearly.

"I don't think so." He spun the ball under one fingertip, seeming more engaged in the activity than the conversation. But that had always been his way. He had frequently disappeared for days in online realms as a kid and had used that skill as a successful game developer. "She looked nervous. Upset. I had the impression she was afraid of getting caught, because she kept glancing over her shoulder."

Miles tried to conjure up a better picture of her from that day when she'd cornered him outside the library. Mostly he remembered that her voice had startled him because it was a girl's, forcing him to look at her more closely since she'd been dressed the same as any of his classmates—jeans, loafers, dark jacket. The clothes must have been borrowed, because they were big on her. Shapeless. Which was probably the point if she wanted to roam freely among them.

Even her hair had been tucked half under a ball cap and half under her coat.

The memory of Chiara's pale face the morning she'd received the threat returned to his brain, reminding him he needed to figure out who would threaten her. Clenching his fist, he pounded it lightly against the window sash before he spoke.

"Who else even knows about Zach?" he asked the group around him, the friends he thought he knew so well. "Let alone would feel threatened if his story came to light?"

For a long moment, the only sounds were the billiard balls Alec knocked against the rails and the sound of ice rattling in Gage's glass. The silence grated Miles's nerves, so he shared his last piece of important news to see if it got his friends talking.

"I'm taking Chiara to the police station after this to let them know about the threats she's receiving, so there's a chance we'll have to answer questions from the authorities about Zach." He knew it went against their longtime promise to protect their friend's memory. But her safety had to come first.

"You would do that?" Alec shook his head and pushed away from the pool table.

Desmond spoke at the same time. "The negative publicity around Mesa Falls is going to have consequences."

From his seat on the leather sofa, Wes shut down the television screen on the wall before he spoke.

"In answer to your question about who else would remember Zach, he was well-known at Dowdon. Teachers and other students all liked him. As for why someone wouldn't want his story to come out…" Wes hesitated, his hazel eyes flicking from one face to the next. "He had a past. And secrets of his own.

Maybe we didn't know Zach as well as we thought we did."

That left the suite even quieter than before. Desmond broke the silence with a soft oath before he leaned over and poured himself a drink from the tray in front of the couch.

The meeting ended with a resolution to convene the next day in the hope they got word from their investigator about Matthew and Nicole Cruz by then. As they began filing out of the suite, Alec and Jonah were still arguing about the idea that they didn't know Zach after all. Miles didn't stick around, not sure what he thought about the possibility.

For now, he needed to see Chiara.

Stalking out of the meeting room, he ran into a young woman hovering around the door. Dressed in leggings and high-top sneakers paired with a blazer, she didn't have the look of a typical casino guest. A red curl fell in her face as she flushed.

"Sorry. Is the meeting over?" she asked, pushing the curl away from her lightly freckled face. As she shifted, her blazer opened to reveal a T-shirt with the characters from Alec's video game. "I'm waiting for Alec—" She glanced over Miles's shoulder. "Is he here?"

Miles nodded but didn't open the door for her since his partners were still discussing Zach. "Just finishing up. He should be out in a minute. Do you work with Alec?"

She hesitated for the briefest moment, a scowl

darkening her features, before she thrust out her hand. "I'm his assistant, Vivian Fraser."

Miles shook it, surprised they hadn't met before. "Miles Rivera. Nice to meet you, Vivian."

Politely, he moved past her, writing off the awkward encounter as his thoughts turned to Chiara.

He'd promised her a date, yes. And the drive to see her was stronger than ever after a meeting that had shaken his foundations. But more importantly, he had questions for her. Questions that couldn't afford to get sidelined by their attraction, no matter how much he wanted to touch her again.

Chiara sent her bodyguard home for the day when she saw Miles approaching the restaurant. Astrid had departed five minutes before, after seeing Jonah's text to meet him in a private suite he'd taken for the rest of their afternoon together.

The new mother had seemed surprised, flustered and adorably excited to have her husband all to herself for a few hours. Chiara had felt a sharp pang of loneliness once she'd left, recognizing that she'd never felt that way about a man. The lack had never bothered her much. Yet between the incredible night she'd spent with Miles and seeing Astrid's happiness transform her, the universe seemed to be conspiring to make her crave romance.

So when Miles slowed his step near the hostess stand of Spice Pavilion, Chiara bristled with defensiveness before he'd even spoken. It didn't help that he was absurdly handsome, impeccably dressed and only had eyes for her, even though he attracted plenty of feminine attention.

"Hello, Chiara." He spoke the greeting with careful deliberation, no doubt emphasizing his good manners after she'd mentioned his habit of skipping the social niceties. "Did you enjoy your lunch?"

She'd been too preoccupied—and maybe a little nervous—about spending more time with him to eat much of anything, but she didn't share that. She rose from the bench where she'd been waiting, restless and needing to move.

"It's always a treat to see Astrid," she told him instead, her slim-cut skirt hugging her thighs as she moved, her body more keenly aware whenever he was near her. "But what about you? Have you eaten?"

She didn't know what went on behind closed doors during a Mesa Falls owners' meeting, but she couldn't envision some of the country's wealthiest men ordering takeout over a conference table. As they walked through the wide corridor that connected the shops to the casino, Chiara dug in her handbag for a pair of sunglasses and slid them into place, hoping to remain unrecognized. The casino crowd was a bit older than her traditional fan base, but she didn't want to risk getting sidetracked from her goal.

"I'm too keyed up to be hungry." Miles took her hand in his, the warmth of his touch encircling her fingers. "Let's take care of reporting the threats against you, and then we need to talk."

She glanced over at him, but his face revealed nothing of his thoughts.

"We're on the same page then." She kept close to him as he increased his pace, cutting through the crowd of tourists, gamblers and locals who visited the Excelsior for a day of entertainment. "Because I hardly touched my lunch for thinking about how much we needed to speak."

He slowed his step just long enough to slant her a sideways glance. "Good. After we take care of the errand at the police station, we can go to your house or my suite. Whichever you prefer for privacy's sake."

The mention of that kind of privacy made her remember what happened when they'd been alone behind closed doors at his home in Mesa Falls. But she agreed. They needed that kind of security for this conversation.

"You have a suite here?" she asked, her heartbeat picking up speed even though they were already heading toward the parking lot, where she guessed Miles had a car waiting.

She suddenly remembered Astrid's face when Jonah had texted her to meet him in a suite for the afternoon. Her friend had lit up from the inside. Chiara had the feeling she looked the exact same way even though her meeting behind closed doors with Miles had a very different purpose.

"I do." His blue gaze was steady as he stopped in the middle of the corridor to let a small troop of feather-clad dancers in matching costumes and sky-high heels glide past them. "Should we go there afterward?"

A whirlwind of questions circled beneath that deceptively simple one. Would she end up in his bed again? Did he want her there? But first and foremost, she needed to know what had happened at the meeting and if Miles had any ideas about who was threatening her.

So she hoped for the best and gave him the only possible response.

"Yes, please."

Eight

Filing a formal complaint with the proper authorities took more time than Chiara would have guessed, which left her more than a little frustrated and exhausted. She hitched her purse up on her shoulder as she charged through the sliding door of the local police station and into a swirl of late-afternoon snow flurries. The whole process had stretched out as Miles spoke to multiple officers at length, eliciting information on possible precautions to take to protect her.

Each cop they'd spoken to had been courteous and professional but not very encouraging that they would be able to help. With the rise of cybercrime, law enforcement was tapped more and more often for infractions committed online, but most local agencies weren't equipped to provide the necessary investigative work. The FBI handled major cases, but at the local level, the best they could do was point her in the direction of the appropriate federal agency, especially considering the threat had targeted Chiara's livelihood and not her person. Still, the importance of the case was increased by the fact that she was a public figure. She'd worked with the local police to file the complaints with the proper federal agencies, and they'd suggested she keep careful records of any problems in the future.

Bottom line, someone would look into it, but chances were good nothing more would come of it unless the threats against her escalated. And thanks to Miles, she wasn't handling this alone.

Chiara glanced back over her shoulder at him as he rebuttoned his suit jacket on their way out the door.

"Thank you for going with me." Chiara held the handrail as she descended the steps outside the municipal building almost three hours after they'd arrived. Her breath huffed visibly in the chilly mountain air as flurries circled them on a gust of wind. "I know it wasn't as satisfying as we might have hoped, but at least we've laid the groundwork if the hacker follows through on his threats."

"Or *her* threats," Miles added, sliding a hand under her elbow and steering her around a patch of ice as they reached the parking lot. "We haven't ruled out a woman's hand in this."

She pulled her coat tighter around her, glad for Miles's support on the slick pavement. The temperature had dropped while they were inside. Then again, thinking about someone threatening her business empire might have been part of the chill she felt. She'd given up her dream of becoming an artist to build the social media presence that had become a formidable brand. That brand was worth all the more to her considering the sacrifices she'd made for it along the way.

"Did you speculate about who might be behind the threats in your meeting today?" she asked, unwilling to delay her questions any longer as they reached his big black Land Rover with snow dusting the hood. "You said you'd share with me what you discussed. And I know Zach's legacy is a concern for you and your friends."

Miles opened the passenger door for her, but before he could reply, a woman's voice called from the next row over in the parking lot.

"Chiara Campagna?"

Distracted, Chiara looked up before thinking the better of it. A young woman dressed in black leggings and a bright pink puffer jacket rushed toward them, her phone lifted as if she was taking a video or a picture.

Miles urged Chiara into the SUV with a nudge, his body blocking anyone from reaching her.

"We should have kept your bodyguard with us," he muttered under his breath as other people on the street outside the municipal building turned toward them.

"Can I get a picture with you?" the woman asked her, already stepping into Miles's personal space and thrusting her phone toward him as she levered between the vehicle and the open door. "I'm such a huge fan."

Chiara put a hand on Miles's arm to let him know it was okay, and he took the phone from the stranger. Chiara knew it might be wiser to leave now before the crowd around them grew, but she'd never been good at disappointing fans. She owed them too much. Yet, in her peripheral vision, she could see a few other people heading toward the vehicle. Impromptu interactions like this could be fun, but they could quickly turn uncomfortable and border-line dangerous.

"Sure," Chiara replied, hoping for the best as she tilted her head toward the other woman's, posing with her and looking into the lens of the camera phone. "But I can only do one," she added, as much for Miles's benefit as the fan's.

Miles took the shot and lowered the phone, appearing to understand her meaning as he met her gaze with those steady blue eyes of his. Without ever looking away from her, he passed the woman in the puffer jacket her phone.

"Ms. Campagna is late for a meeting," he explained, inserting himself between Chiara and the fan before shifting his focus to the other woman. "She appreciates your support, but I need to deliver her to her next appointment now."

He backed the other woman away, closing and locking the SUV's passenger door just in time, as two teenaged boys clambered over to bang on the vehicle's hood and shout her name, their phones raised.

The noise made her tense, but Chiara slid her sunglasses onto her nose and kept her head down. She dug in her bag for her own phone, hoping she wouldn't need to call Stefan for assistance. She'd been in situations with crowds that had turned aggressive before, and the experiences had terrified her. She knew all too well how fast things could escalate.

But a moment later, the clamor outside the SUV eased enough for Miles to open the driver's door and slide into his own seat. She peered through the windshield then, spotting a uniformed police officer disbanding the gathering onlookers who had quickly multiplied in number. The teenaged boys were legging it down the street. The woman in the puffer jacket was showing her phone to a group of other ladies, gesturing excitedly with her other hand. People had gathered to see what was happening, stepping out of businesses in a strip mall across the parking lot.

"I'm sorry about that." Miles turned on the engine and backed out of the parking space. He gave a wave to the officer through the windshield. "Does that happen often?"

"Not lately," she admitted, shaken at the close call. "I've gotten better in the last year about wearing hats and sunglasses, keeping security near me, and having my outings really scripted so that I'm never in public for long."

She'd been so distracted ever since spending the night with Miles that she was forgetting to take precautions. She pressed farther back in her seat, ready to retreat from the world.

"That doesn't sound like a fun way to live." He steered the vehicle out of the parking lot and started driving away from town. "And now that news of your presence here has no doubt been plastered all over the web, I'd like to take you to the villa you rented instead of the resort. It will be quieter there."

"That's fine." She appreciated the suggestion as the snow began falling faster. "I'll message Stefan—he's my head of security—and ask him to bring in some more help for the rest of my stay."

"Good." Miles nodded his approval of the plan, his square jaw flexing. "Until we find out who's been threatening you, it pays to take extra safety measures."

She drew a deep breath, needing to find a way to reroute this conversation. To return to her goal for this time with Miles, which was to learn more about what happened to Zach. But she hadn't quite recovered from the near miss with fans who could turn from warmhearted supporters to angry detractors with little to no warning. It only took a few people in a crowd to change the mood or to start shoving.

"Or…" Miles seemed to muse aloud as he drove, the quiet in the car all the more pronounced as they left the more populated part of the lakeshore behind them.

When he didn't seem inclined to finish his thought, Chiara turned to look at him again, but she couldn't read his expression, which veered between a frown and thoughtful contemplation.

"Or what?" she prodded him, curious what was on his mind.

"I was just going to say that if you decide at any time you would prefer more seclusion, my ranch in the Sierra Nevada foothills is open to you." He glanced her way as he said it.

"Rivera Ranch?" She knew it was his family seat, the property he invested the majority of his time in running.

The invitation surprised her. First of all, because Miles seemed like an intensely private man, the most reserved of the Mesa Falls owners. He didn't strike her as the kind of person to open his home to many people. Secondly, she wouldn't have guessed that she would rank on the short list of people he would welcome.

"Yes." His thumbs drummed softly against the steering wheel. "It's remote. The property is gated and secure. You'd be safe there."

"Alone?" The word slipped out before she could catch it.

"Only if you chose to be. I'm happy to escort you. At least until you got settled in."

The offer was thoughtful, if completely unexpected. Still, it bore consideration if the threats against her kept escalating.

"I hope it doesn't come to that," she told him truthfully. "But thank you."

"Just remember you have options." He turned on the long private drive that led to her villa on the lake. "You're not in this alone."

She was tempted to argue that point. To tell him she felt very much alone in her quest to learn more about Zach since Miles refused to talk about their mutual friend. But he was here with her now. And he'd said they needed to help each other. Maybe he was ready to break his long silence at last.

Yet somehow that seemed less important than the prospect of spending time alone with this man who tempted her far too much.

Miles recognized the couple waiting in front of Chiara's villa as he parked the vehicle. The tall, athletic-looking brunette was Chiara's assistant, and the burly dude dressed all in black had been Chiara's bodyguard the night of the party at Mesa Falls Ranch. The two held hands, wearing matching tense expressions. They broke apart when Miles halted the vehicle but still approached the passenger door as a team.

"They must have seen photos from the police department parking lot online." Chiara sighed in frustration as she unbuckled her seat belt and clutched her handbag. "I'll just need a minute to bring them up to speed."

"Of course." Miles nodded at the muscle-bound man who opened Chiara's door for her. "Take your time. I'll check out your lake view to give you some privacy."

"That's not necessary," she protested, allowing her bodyguard to help her down from the vehicle.

Opening his own door, Miles discovered the tall assistant was waiting on his side of the Land Rover. Meeting her brown eyes, he remembered her name from the party at Mesa Falls.

"Hi, Jules," he greeted the woman, who had to be six feet tall even in her flat-soled running shoes. She wore a sweater and track pants, seemingly unconcerned with the cold. "Nice to see you again."

"You, too." She gave him a quick smile, but it was plain she had other things on her mind. A furrow between her brows deepened before she lowered her voice to speak to him quietly. "I wanted to warn you that while you were out with Chiara today, you attracted the interest of some of her fans."

"Should I be concerned?" He stepped down to the pavement beside her while, near the rear of the

SUV, Chiara related the story of what happened at the police department to her security guard.

"Not necessarily." Jules hugged her arms around her waist, breathing a white cloud into the cold air. "But since Chiara's fan base can be vocal and occasionally unpredictable, you should probably alert your PR team to keep an eye on the situation."

"I'm a rancher," he clarified, amused. He stuffed his hands in his pockets to ward off the chill of the day. "I don't have a PR team."

"Mesa Falls has a dedicated staffer," she reminded him, switching on the tablet she was holding. A gust of wind caught her long ponytail and blew it all around her. "I remember because I dealt with her directly about the party at your place. Would you like me to contact her about this instead?"

Puzzled, Miles watched the woman swipe through several screens before pausing on an avatar of the Montana ranch.

"Just what do you think could happen?" he asked her, curious about the potential risks of dating someone famous.

If, in fact, what they were doing together could even be called dating. His gaze slanted over to Chiara, who was heading toward the front door of the villa, flashes of her long legs visible from the opening of her coat. He realized he wanted more with her. At very least, he wanted a repeat of their incredible night together. Preferably, he wanted many repeats of that night.

Beside him, Chiara's assistant huffed out a sigh that pulled him back to their conversation.

"Anything could happen," Jules told him flatly as she frowned. "You could become a target for harassment or worse. Your home address could be made public, and you could find yourself or your family surrounded in your own home. Your business could be boycotted if Chiara's fans decide they don't like you. People have no idea how brutal it can be in the public eye."

She sounded upset. Miles wondered what kinds of things Chiara had weathered in the past because of her fame.

He felt his eyebrows rise even as the idea worried him more for Chiara's sake than his own. "I appreciate the warning. If you don't mind sending a message to the Mesa Falls publicity person, I'd appreciate it."

"Of course." She nodded, tapping out some notes on her tablet even as snowflakes fell and melted on the screen. "And you should consider security for yourself once you leave the villa. At least for the next week or so until we know how the story plays out."

"I'll consider it," he assured her, sensing it would be better to placate her for now, or until he had a better handle on the situation for himself. He didn't want to rile Chiara's assistant when the woman already seemed upset. "Did today's incident cause problems for you?"

Jules shoved her tablet under her arm again. "For me personally? Not yet. But having her photographed in front of a police station is already causing speculation that we'll have to figure out how to address."

He nodded, beginning to understand how small missteps like today could have a big impact on Chiara's carefully planned public image. "I should have taken steps to ensure she wasn't recognized."

A wry smile curved the woman's lips. "Bingo."

"I can't fix what already happened today, but I can promise I'll take better care of her in the future," he assured the woman, gesturing her toward the house.

Jules pivoted on the heel of her tennis shoe and walked with him toward the stone steps at the side entrance. "If she keeps you around, I would appreciate that."

Miles chucked softly as he opened the front door for her. "Do you think my days are numbered with her after this?"

"No. Well, not because of today. But Chiara is notoriously choosy when it comes to the men in her life." She lowered her voice as they crossed the threshold of the huge lakefront house.

From the foyer, Miles could see Chiara standing with her bodyguard in the kitchen. Behind her, the setting sun glittered on the lake outside the floor-to-ceiling windows.

"That's a good thing." Miles was damned choosy himself. Until Chiara, he hadn't let any woman close to him for more than a night ever since he'd accidentally ended up dating the same woman as his brother. "I admire a woman with discriminating taste."

Jules laughed. "Then maybe you two have more in common than I would have guessed. I've worked with Chiara for three years, and you're the first man she's ever changed her schedule for."

He wanted to ask her what she meant by that, but as soon as the words were out, Chiara entered the foyer alone. Something about the way she carried herself told him she was upset. Or maybe it was the expression on her face, the worry in her eyes. And damned if he hadn't spent enough time studying her to recognize the subtle shift of her moods.

"Jules." Chiara still wore her long coat, her arms wrapped around herself as if she was chilled. "Stefan went out the back to the guesthouse, but he said he'll meet you out front if you still want to head into town."

Jules looked back and forth between them, but then her attention locked in on Chiara, perhaps seeing the same stress that Miles had noted. Jules stroked her friend's hair where it rested on her shoulder. "I don't want to go anywhere if you need me."

Miles wondered if he'd missed something. If the photos online were a bigger deal than he was understanding. Or was it his presence causing the added stress?

"I can take off if this is a bad time," he offered, unwilling to stay if they needed to take care of other things. He'd come a long way from the guy who'd written off Chiara's job as glorified partying, but no doubt he still didn't understand the nuances of her work, let alone the ramifications of the day's unexpected encounter with her fans.

Chiara's green eyes lifted to his. "No. I'd like to talk." Then she turned to her assistant and squeezed Jules's hand. "I'm fine. But thank you. I want you to have fun tonight. You work too hard."

"It never feels like work for me when we're hanging out," the other woman insisted before she gave a nod. "But if you're sure you don't mind—"

"I insist." Chiara walked toward the oversize door with her. "Stefan already has two guards watching the house tonight, and Miles will be here with me for a few more hours."

He couldn't help but hope that boded well for their evening together. Although maybe Chiara was just trying to soothe her friend's anxiety about leaving her.

In another moment, Jules departed, and the house was vacant except for the two of them. The sound of the door shutting echoed from the cathedral ceiling in the foyer. Chiara took a moment to check that the alarm reset before she turned toward him again.

"May I take your coat?" he asked, moving closer to her.

Wanting to touch her, yes. But wanting to comfort her, too.

She looked down at what she was wearing and shook her head, clearly having forgotten that she'd left her coat on.

"Oh. Thank you." She sucked in a breath as he

stepped behind her and rested his hands on her shoulders for a moment. "I think I got a chill while we were out."

"Or maybe it's the combination of dealing with the threats, the police and the work crisis that seems to have snowballed from having our photo taken today." He took hold of the soft wool and cashmere cloak and helped her slide it from her arms.

The movement shifted her dark waves of hair and stirred her citrusy scent. He breathed it in, everything about her affecting him. As much as he wanted to turn her toward him and kiss her, he realized he wanted to ease her worries even more. So after hanging the coat on a wooden peg just inside the mudroom off the foyer, he returned to her side, resting his hand lightly on her spine to steer her toward the living room.

"You're probably right. The police station visit would have been daunting enough without the drama afterward." She shivered and hugged her arms tighter around herself.

Miles led her to the sofa, moving aside a throw pillow to give her the comfortable corner seat. Then he pulled a plush blanket off the sofa back and draped it around her before finding the fireplace remote and switching on the flames. The blinds in the front room were already drawn, but he pulled the heavy curtains over them, too.

Then he took a seat on the wide ottoman, shoving aside a tray full of design books and coasters to make more room.

"May I take these off for you?" He gestured toward the high leather boots she was still wearing.

Her lips lifted on one side. "Really?" A sparkle returned to her green eyes, a flare of interest or anticipation. At least, he hoped that's what it was. "If you don't mind."

"I want to make you comfortable. And I don't want you to regret sending away your friends tonight." He lowered the zipper on the first boot, reminding himself he was only doing this to help her relax. Not to seduce her.

Although skimming his hand lightly over the back of her calf as he removed the boot was doing a hell of a job of seducing *him*.

"I won't." Her gaze locked on his hands where he touched her. "I've been anxious to talk to you all day."

The reminder that this wasn't a real date came just in time as Miles eased off the second boot. Because he'd been tempted to stroke back up her leg to her knee.

And linger there.

Even now, the hem of her skirt just above her knee was calling to him. But first, they needed to address the topic he'd avoided for fourteen years.

Damn it.

With an effort, he set aside her footwear and released her leg. Then he took the seat next to her on the couch.

"Okay." He braced himself, remembering that his friends hadn't been any help today. It was time to break the silence. "Let's talk."

"I have a question I've been wanting to ask you." Reaching beneath the blanket, Chiara shifted to gain access to a pocket on the front of her houndstooth skirt. She withdrew a piece of paper and smoothed it out to show him a grainy photo. "Do you know who this is, Miles?"

He glanced down at the photo, and passion faded as suspicion iced everything he'd been feeling. Apparently Chiara wasn't stopping her quest for answers about Zach. Because the face staring back at Miles from the image was someone he and Zach had both known well. And he couldn't begin to guess why Chiara wanted to know about her.

Nine

Chiara didn't miss the flare of recognition in Miles's eyes as he looked at the yearbook photo.

"You're pointing at this woman in the background?" he asked, stabbing the paper with his index finger.

"The one with the side part and the navy blue skirt," she clarified. "She doesn't look like a student."

"She wasn't. That's Miss Allen, one of the student teachers at Dowdon." He met her gaze as he smiled. "Lana Allen. We were all a little in love with her."

"A teacher?" Shock rippled through her, followed by cold, hard dread. "Are you sure? She's not in the yearbook anywhere else. How old do you think she was?"

Miles must have read some of her dismay, because his expression went wary. He tensed beside her on the sofa.

"There was major backlash about her being at our school since she was just nineteen herself. She didn't stay the full year at Dowdon after one of the administrators complained she was a distraction. She worked with Alonzo Salazar briefly during the fall semester and then she was gone—" His jaw flexed as if mulling over how much to say. "Before Christmas break. Why?"

Her stomach knotted at the implications of what this new revelation meant. She hoped it wasn't a mistake to confide in him. But if one of them didn't take the leap and start sharing information, they'd never figure out who was harassing her or what it had to do with Zach.

Taking a deep breath, she sat up straighter and told him. "I saw Zach kissing her. As in a real, no-holds-barred, passionate kiss."

Miles shook his head then gripped his temples between his thumb and forefinger, squeezing. "Impossible. It must have been someone else."

"No." She was certain. How many times had she relived that moment in her mind over the years? "Miles, I had the biggest crush on him. I followed him around like the lovesick teenager I was, just hoping for the chance to talk to him alone. I never would have mistaken him for someone else."

"Then you're confused about her," he insisted. "It was a long time ago, Chiara, how can you be sure—"

"I picked her face out of the background crowd in this photo just like that." She snapped her fingers. "The memory has been burned into my brain for fourteen years, because it broke my heart to see that Zach already had a girlfriend."

"She couldn't have been his girlfriend—"

"His romantic interest, then," she amended, staring into the flames flickering in the fireplace as she tucked her feet beneath her and pulled the plush throw blanket tighter around her legs. "Or hers, I guess, since she was a legal adult by then and he was still technically a kid." The woman had no business touching a student, damn it. The idea made her ill.

"Zach was older than us—seventeen when he died. But obviously that doesn't excuse her. If anything, the relationship gives a probable cause for Zach's unhappiness before he died." His scowl deepened.

A fresh wave of regret wrenched her insides at the thought of Zach hurting that much. "I saw them together at the art show where Zach and I were both exhibiting work. I couldn't find him anywhere, so I finally went outside looking for them, and they were hidden in one of the gardens, arms wound around each other—"

She broke off, the memory still stinging. Not because of the romantic heartbreak—she'd gotten over that in time. But she'd left the art show after that, turning her back on Zach when he'd called after her. Little did she know she'd never see him again. Remembering that part still filled her with guilt.

Miles studied her face, seeming content to wait for her to finish, even as he saw too much. When she didn't speak, he reached between them to thread his fingers through hers. The warmth of his touch—the kindness of it—stole her breath. He'd been an anchor for her on a hard day, and she didn't have a chance of refusing the steadiness he offered.

"Okay. Assuming you're correct, why would Zach tell us he was gay if he wasn't?"

"He might have been confused. Fourteen years ago there wasn't as much discussion about sexuality, so he could have misidentified himself." Although he'd always seemed so sure of himself in other ways... She remembered how mature Zach had been. "Or maybe he thought he was protecting her—misdirecting people so no one suspected their relationship."

Miles seemed to consider this for a moment.

"But he told us over the summer," Miles argued. "We had a group video call before the semester even started, and he told us then."

"Zach and I were both at school all summer," she reminded him. "For our art program. Lana Allen could have been around Dowdon during the summer months, too."

Miles swore softly under his breath, and she wondered if that meant he was conceding her point.

He dragged a hand over his face and exhaled as he turned to look her in the eye. His thigh grazed her knee where her legs were folded beneath her, the contact sizzling its way up her hip.

"This is huge." He squeezed her palm, his thumb rubbing lightly over the back of her hand. "It changes everything."

"How so?" She went still, hoping he was finally going to trust her enough to share the truth about Zach's death.

He looked uneasy. Then, taking a deep breath, he said, "For starters, I think Zach might have a son."

The news was so unexpected it took her a moment to absorb what he was saying.

"By this woman?" she wondered aloud, doing the math in her head. Zach had been seventeen at the time, and he'd died fourteen years ago. His son would be at least thirteen by now. "Why? Have you seen her?"

"No." Releasing her hand, Miles rose to his feet as if seized by a new restless energy. He massaged the back of his neck while he paced the great room. When he reached the windows overlooking the mountains, he pivoted hard on the rug and stalked toward her again. "A woman came to Mesa Falls a few months ago claiming to have custody of her sister's child—a thirteen-year-old boy of unknown paternity. The mother died suddenly of an aneurysm and had never told anyone who the father was."

Chiara hugged herself as she focused on his

words. "And that's the child you think could be Zach's son?"

He nodded. "The woman claimed the kid's upbringing was being funded by profits from *Hollywood Newlyweds*. At the time, we wondered if the child could have been one of ours, since Alonzo had helped us all through the aftermath of Zach's death. He was a mentor for all of us."

She covered her lips to smother a gasp of surprise as new pieces fell into place. The news that a private school English teacher had been the pseudonymous author behind *Hollywood Newlyweds* had been splashed everywhere over Christmas, sending tabloid journalists scrambling to piece together why the author had never taken credit for the book before his death. It made sense to her that he would keep it a secret if he was using the profits to help Zach's son.

Aloud, she mused, "You think Salazar knew about Zach's son and was trying to funnel some funds to the mother to help raise the baby?"

"Since Lana Allen was his student teacher, maybe he discovered the affair at some point. Although if he knew and didn't report her to the authorities— *hell*. Maybe he felt guilty for not intervening sooner." Miles stopped at the other end of the great room, where Chiara had left her sketchbook. He traced a finger over the open page. "It's all speculation, but you can see where I'm going with this."

Her mind was spinning with the repercussions of the news, and she wasn't sure what it meant for the friends Zach had left behind. For her. For Miles. And all the other owners of Mesa Falls Ranch. Was this the secret her hacker was trying to steer her away from finding? And if so, why?

Needing a break from the revelations coming too fast to process, she slid off her throw blanket and rose to join Miles near the table that held her sketchbook. For the moment, it felt easier to think about something else than to wade through what she'd just learned.

So instead, she wondered what he thought of her drawings. She couldn't seem to give up her love of art even though she'd ended up working in a field that didn't call for many of the skills she wished she was using.

Yet another question about Zach's son bubbled to the surface, and she found herself asking, "Where is the boy now? And the woman who is guarding him—his aunt? She might have the answers we need."

Miles spoke absently as he continued to peruse the sketches. "We have a private detective following a lead on them now. We discussed this at yesterday's meeting, but I don't know if the lead panned out yet." He pulled his attention away from her drawings to meet her gaze. "These are yours?"

She suspected he needed a break from the thoughts about Zach as much as she did.

"Yes." Her gaze followed the familiar lines of pencil drawings from long ago. She'd been carry-

ing around the sketchbook ever since her days at
Brookfield, hoping that seeing the drawings now
and then would keep her focused on her quest to
find out what happened to Zach. Seeing them now
helped her to say to Miles, "You're welcome to look
at them, but I wish you'd tell me about the day Zach
died. I know you were with him."

She'd learned long ago that the Mesa Falls Ranch
owners had all been on a horseback riding trip that
weekend. She knew seven riders had left Dowdon
but only six had returned.

The firelight cast flickering shadows on Miles's
face as he flipped a page in the sketchbook, revealing a cartoonish horse in muted charcoals. He must
have recognized the image, because his expression
changed when he saw it.

"This horse looks like the one in Alec's video
game," he noted, the comment so off-topic from what
she'd asked that she could only think Miles wasn't
ready to talk about it.

Frustrated, she shook her head but let him lead
her back to the discussion of the drawings.

"No." She pointed at the image over his shoulder,
the warmth of his body making her wish she could
lean into him. "That's a favorite image of Zach's. The
horse motif was really prevalent in his work over the
four months before he died." She thought she'd done
a faithful job of copying the sort of figure Zach had
sketched so often. He'd inspired her in so many ways.
"Why? What does it have to do with a video game?"

Miles's brow furrowed. "Alec Jacobsen—one of my partners—is a game developer. The series he created using this horse as a character is his most popular."

How had she missed that? She made a mental note to look for the game.

"Then Zach's work must have inspired him," she said firmly, knowing that her friend had worked similar images into most of his dreamlike paintings.

"No doubt. Those two were close friends. I think Alec credited Zach somewhere on his debut game." He flipped another page in the book while a grandfather clock in the foyer struck the hour with resonant chimes. "As for how Zach died, it's still disputed among us."

Her nerve endings tingled to hear the words. To realize she was close to finally learning the truth after all this time. She held her breath. Waiting. Hoping he would confide in her.

Miles never took his gaze from the sketchbook as he spoke again. Quietly.

"He jumped off one of the cliffs into the Arroyo Seco River on a day after heavy rainstorms that raised the water level significantly." He dragged in a slow breath for a moment before he continued. "But we were never sure if he jumped for fun, because he was a daredevil who lived on the edge, or if he made that leap with the intent to end his life."

Chiara closed her eyes, picturing the scene. Zach has been a boy of boundless energy. Big dreams.

Big emotions. She could see him doing something so reckless, and she hurt all over again to imagine him throwing everything away in one poor decision.

"He drowned?" Her words were so soft, they felt like they'd been spoken by someone else.

"He never surfaced. They found the body later downstream." Miles paused a moment, setting down the sketchbook and dragging in a breath. "Since there were no suspicious circumstances, they didn't do an autopsy. His death certificate lists drowning as the cause of death."

"How could it not be suspicious?" she asked, her heart rate kicking up. She felt incensed that no one had investigated further. "Even now, you don't know what happened for sure."

"The accident was kept quiet since suicide was a possibility. And Zach had no family."

"Meaning there was no one to fight for justice for him," she remarked bitterly, knowing from personal experience how difficult it had been to find out anything. "So the school ensured no one found out that a fatal incident occurred involving Dowdon students."

The bleakness in his eyes was impossible to miss. "That's right." His nod was stiff. Unhappy. "On the flip side, there was concern about the rest of us. We were all shell-shocked."

Something in his voice, the smallest hesitation from a man normally so confident, forced her to step back. To really listen to what he was saying and remember that this wasn't just about Zach. What happened on that trip had left its mark on Miles and all of his friends.

"I'm sorry," she offered quietly, threading her fingers through his the way he had earlier. "It must have been awful for you."

"We all went in the water to look for him," he continued, his blue gaze fixed on a moment in the past she couldn't see. "Wes could have died—he jumped right in after him. The rest of us climbed down to the rocks below to see if we could find him."

For a long moment, they didn't speak. She stepped closer, tipping her head to his shoulder in wordless comfort.

"Time gets fuzzy after that. I don't know how we decided to quit looking, but it took a long time. We were all frozen—inside and out. Eventually, we rode back to get help, but by then we knew no one was going to find him. At least—" his chin dropped to rest on the top of her head "—not alive."

Her chest ached at the thought of sixteen-year-old Miles searching a dangerously churning river for his friend and not finding him. She couldn't imagine how harrowing the aftermath had been. She'd grappled with Zach's loss on her own, not knowing the circumstances of his death. But for Miles to witness his friend's last moments like that, feeling guilt about it no matter how misplaced, had to be an unbearable burden. A lifelong sorrow.

Helpless to know what to say, she stepped into him, wrapping her arms around his waist. She tucked her forehead against his chest, feeling the rhythmic beat of his heart against her ear. She breathed in the scent of him—clean laundry and a hint of spice from his aftershave. Her hands traced the contours of his strong arms, the hard plane of his chest and ridged abs.

At his quick intake of breath, she glanced up in time to see his eyes darken. Her heart rate sped faster.

Miles cupped her chin, bringing her mouth closer to his.

"I never talk about this because it hurts too damned much." His words sounded torn out of him.

"Thank you for trusting me enough to tell me." She'd waited half her life to hear what had happened to her friend. "At least he wasn't alone."

"No. He wasn't." Miles stroked his fingers through her hair, sifting through the strands to cup the back of her head and draw her closer still. "Any one of us would have died to save him. That's how close we were."

She'd never had friendships like that when she was a teen. Only later, once she met Astrid and then Jules, did she feel like she had people in her life who would have her back no matter what. Could she trust what Miles said about his love for Zach? She still wondered at his motives for keeping the details of Zach's death private. But as she drew a breath to ask about that, Miles gently pressed his finger against her mouth.

"I promise we can talk about this more," he told her, dragging the digit along her lower lip. "But first, I need a minute." He wrapped his other arm around her waist, his palm settling into the small of her back to seal their bodies together. "Or maybe I just need you."

Miles tipped his forehead to Chiara's, letting the sensation of having her in his arms override the dark churn of emotions that came from talking about the most traumatic day of his life. He felt on edge. Guilt-ridden. Defensive as hell.

He should have been at Zach's side when he jumped. He knew the guy was on edge that weekend. They'd stayed up half the night talking, and he'd known that something was off. Of course, they'd *all* known something was off since Zach had initiated the unsanctioned horseback riding trip precisely because he was pissed off and wanted to get away from school.

But he'd hinted at something bigger than the usual problems while they'd talked and drank late into the night. Miles had never been able to remember the conversation clearly, since they'd been drinking. The night only came back to him in jumbled bits that left him feeling even guiltier that he hadn't realized Zach was battling big demons.

Miles had still been hungover the morning of the cliff-jumping accident. He hadn't wanted to go in the first place because of that, and he sure as hell hadn't been as clearheaded as he should have been while they'd trekked up the trail. He'd lagged behind the whole way, and by the time he realized that Zach had jumped despite the dangerous conditions, Miles's brother was already throwing himself off the precipice to find him.

His brain stuttered on that image—the very real fear his brother wouldn't surface, either. And it stuck there.

Until Chiara shifted in his arms, her hips swaying against him in a way that recalibrated everything. His thoughts. His mood. His body. All of his focus narrowed to her. This sexy siren of a woman who fascinated him on every level.

Possessiveness surged through him along with hunger. Need.

A need for her. A need to forget.

He edged back to see her, taking in the spill of dark hair and mossy-green eyes full of empathy and fire, too. When her gaze dipped to his mouth, it was all he could do not to taste her. Lose himself in her.

But damn it, he needed her to acknowledge that she wanted this, too.

"I could kiss you all night long." He stroked along her jaw, fingers straying to the delicate underside of her chin where her skin was impossibly soft.

He trailed a touch down the long column of her throat and felt the gratifying thrum of her pulse racing there. He circled the spot with his thumb and then traced it with his tongue.

"Then why don't you?" she asked, her breathless words sounding dry and choked.

"I can't even talk you into the date you owe me." He angled her head so he could read her expression better in the light of the fire. Her silky hair brushed the back of his hand. "It seems presumptuous of me to seduce you."

"Not really." She tilted her face so that her cheek rubbed against the inside of his wrist, her eyelids falling to half-mast as she did it, as if just that innocent touch brought her pleasure.

Hell, it brought him pleasure, too. But then his brain caught up to her words.

"It wouldn't be presumptuous?" he asked, wanting her to take ownership of this attraction flaring so hot between them he could feel the flames licking up his legs.

"No." Her breath tickled against his forearm before she kissed him there then nipped his skin lightly between her teeth. "Not when being with you is all I think about every night."

The admission slayed him, torching his reservations, because *damn*. He thought about her that much, too. More.

"Good." He arched her neck back even farther, ready to claim her mouth. "That's...good."

His lips covered hers, and she was even softer than he remembered, sweetly yielding. Her arms slid around him, her body melting into his, breasts molding to his chest. He could feel the tight points of her nipples right through her blouse and the thin fabric of her bra. It felt like forever since he'd seen her. Held her. Stripped off her clothes and buried himself inside her.

He couldn't wait to do all those things, but he wouldn't do them here in the middle of the living room. With someone tracking her activities, he wanted as many locked doors between them and the rest of the world as possible. He needed her safe. Naked and sighing his name as he pleasured her, yes.

But above all, safe.

Breaking the kiss, he spoke into her ear. "Take me to your bedroom. Our night is about to get a whole lot better."

Ten

Chiara didn't hesitate.

She wanted Miles with a fierceness she didn't begin to understand, but ever since their one incredible night together, she'd been longing for a repeat. Maybe a part of her hoped that she'd embellished it in her mind, and that the sizzling passion had been a result of other factors at work that night. That it was a result of her nervousness at being caught in his office. Or her fascination with meeting one of Zach's closest friends.

But based on the way she was already trembling for want of Miles, she knew her memory of their night together was as amazing as she remembered. Wordlessly, she pulled him by the hand through the sprawling villa. At the top of the split staircase, she veered to the right, where the master suite dominated the back of the house.

She drew him into the spacious room, where he paused to close the door and lock it, a gesture that felt symbolic more than anything, since they were the only ones home. The soft *snick* of the lock sent a shiver through her as she flipped on the light switch and dimmed the overhead fixture. A gas fire burned in the stone hearth in the wall opposite the bed, and even though the flames lit the room, she liked to have the overhead light on to see Miles better. She watched him wander deeper into the room to the doors overlooking the lake. He shrugged off his blue suit jacket and laid it over the back of a leather wingback by the French doors. Picking up the control for the blinds, he closed them all and turned to look at her.

With his fitted shirt skimming his shoulders, it was easy to appreciate his very male physique. Her gaze dropped lower, sidetracked by the sight of still *more* maleness. All for her.

She wanted him, but it felt good to know he wanted her every bit as much. She dragged in breath like she'd just run a race. Heat crawled up her spine while desire pooled in her belly.

After a moment, Miles beckoned to her. "You're too far away for us to have as much fun as I was hoping."

The rasp of his voice smoked through her. Anticipation spiked, making her aware of her heart-beat pulsing in unexpected erogenous zones. But she didn't move closer. She lifted her gaze, though, meeting his blue eyes over the king-size bed.

"Give me a moment to take it all in. The first time we were together, I didn't get to appreciate all the details." In her dreams, she'd feverishly recreated every second with him, but there were too many gaps in her memories. How his hair felt in her fingers, for example. Or the texture of his very capable hands. "Tonight, I'm savoring everything."

As soon as she said it, she realized it made her sound like she was falling for him. She wanted to re-cant the words. To say what she meant another way. But if Miles noticed, he didn't comment. Instead he turned his attention to unbuttoning his shirt.

"I like the way you think." His lips curved in a half smile. "But if I'm going to show you all my *details* to savor, I hope you plan to do the same."

She knew she should just be grateful for the out—he hadn't taken her words to mean anything seri-ous. And she hadn't meant them that way. But now that the idea was out there in the ether, she had to acknowledge that it rattled her. Worried her. She couldn't fall for Miles.

Could she?

A swish of material jolted her attention back to Miles's shirt falling to the floor. His chest and abs were burnished gold by the firelight, the ripples of

muscle highlighted by the shadowed ridges in between them. She wanted to focus on him. On them.

"Chiara." He said her name as he charged toward
her. "What's wrong?"

His hands slid around her waist. Bracketed her
hips. The warmth of his body rekindled her heat despite her spiraling thoughts.

"Is it crazy for us to indulge this?" She steadied
herself by gripping his upper arms, and he felt so
good. Solid. Warm.

Like he was hers.

For tonight, at least.

"Why would it be?" He frowned as he planted his
feet wider to bring himself closer to her eye level.
"What could possibly be wrong with finding pleasure together after the day you've had? Your business has been threatened, but the cops won't help.
I'm scared as hell that you could be vulnerable, and
yet you don't want to let me get too close to you or
take care of you."

The urge to lean into him, to let him do just that,
was almost overwhelming. But she had to be honest,
even if it doused the flame for him. "Trust comes
hard for me."

Her parents hadn't bothered to tell her when they
lost their fortune. Zach had kept secrets from her.
Miles kept secrets, too. Although he *had* confided
more to her tonight.

"Which is why I haven't pushed you to stay with
me so I can protect you. But you told me yourself

that you thought about being with me every night."
His hands flexed against her where he held her hips,
a subtle pressure that stirred sweet sensations. "So
maybe you could at least trust me to make you feel
good."

"I do." She swayed closer, telling herself she could
have one more night with him without losing her
heart. "I have absolute faith in that."

He gripped the silk of her blouse at her waist and
slowly gathered the fabric, untucking the shirttail
from her skirt.

"I'm glad. Remember when you told me you chose
work over fun for a long time?" he asked, leaning
closer to speak into her ear. And to nip her ear with
his teeth.

A shiver coursed through her along with surprise
that he recalled her words. "Y-yes."

"That ends now."

Miles kissed his way down her neck, smoothing
aside her thick, dark hair to taste more of her. She
needed this as much as he did. Maybe even more.

It stunned him to think he read her so clearly
when they'd spent so little time together, but he recognized how hard she pushed herself. How much
she demanded of herself even when her world was
caving in around her. The devotion of her staff—all
personal friends, apparently—spoke volumes about
who she was, and it made him want to take care of

her, if only for tonight. He was going to help her forget all about her burdens until she lost herself in this.

In him.

Not that he was being unselfish. Far from it. He craved this woman.

Flicking open the buttons on her blouse, he nudged the thin fabric off her shoulders and let it flutter to the floor before he lifted his head to study her in the glow of the firelight.

"Are you still with me?" He followed the strap of her ivory lace bra with his fingertip.

The dark fringe of her eyelashes wavered before she glanced up at him, green eyes filled with heat. "Definitely."

The answer cranked him higher. He raked the straps from her shoulders and unhooked the lace to free her. The soft swells of her breasts spilled into his waiting hands, stirring the citrus fragrance he'd come to associate with her.

Hauling her into his arms, he lifted her, taking his time so that her body inched slowly up the length of his. He walked her to the bed and settled her in the space between the rows of pillows at the head and the down comforter folded at the foot, her hair spread out behind her like a silky halo. She followed his movements with watchful green eyes as he unfastened the side zipper of her skirt and eased it down her hips, leaving her in nothing but a scrap of ivory lace.

She made an enticing picture on the bed while he removed the rest of his own clothes. When he paused in undressing to find a condom and place it on the bed near her, she kinked a finger into the waistband of his boxers and tugged lightly.

"You're not naked enough." She grazed a touch along his abs, making his muscles jump with the featherlight caress.

"I'm working on it," he assured her, stilling her questing hand before she distracted him from his goal. "But we're taking care of you first."

"We are?" Her breath caught as he leaned over her and kneed her thighs apart to make room for himself.

The mattress dipped beneath them, their bodies swaying together.

"Ladies first." He kissed her hip, and she arched beneath him. "Call me old-fashioned."

He slid his hand beneath the ivory lace and stroked the slick heat waiting for him there. Her only reply was a soft gasp, followed by a needy whimper that told him she was already close.

She sifted her fingers through his hair, wriggling beneath him as he kissed and teased her, taking her higher and then easing back until they were both hot and edgy. The third time he felt her breathing shift, her thighs tensing, he didn't stop. He fastened his lips to her as she arched against him, and with a hard shudder, she flew apart.

He helped her ride out the sensations, relishing every buck of her hips, every soft shiver of her damp flesh. When he kissed his way back up her torso, he stopped at her breasts to pay homage to each in turn.

Chiara patted around the bed for the condom and, finding it, rolled it into place. The feel of her hands on him, that efficient stroke of her fingers, nearly cost him his restraint. He closed his eyes against the heat jolting through him.

"Your turn," she whispered huskily in his ear before she gently bit his shoulder. "I'm in charge."

She pushed against his shoulder until he flipped onto his back. When she straddled him, her dark hair trailed along his chest while she made herself comfortable. Her green eyes seemed to dare him to argue as she arched an eyebrow at him.

But Miles couldn't have denied her a damn thing she wanted. Not now, when her cheeks were flushed with color, her nipples dark and thrusting from his touch. The glow of the chandelier brought out the copper highlights in her raven-colored hair. He caught her hips in his hands, steadying her as she poised herself above him.

Their eyes met, held, as he lowered her onto him. Everything inside him stilled, the sensation of being inside her better than any feeling he'd ever known.

Damn.

He cranked his eyes closed long enough to get command of himself. To grind his teeth against the way this woman was stealing into his life and rewiring his brain. When he opened his eyes again, he sat up, wrapping his arms around her waist to take her to the edge of the bed so she was seated on his lap.

They were even this way. Face-to-face. They had equal amounts of control.

He told himself that with every thrust. Every breath. Every heartbeat. They moved together in sweet, sensual harmony. Their bodies anticipating one another, pushing each other higher. She held on to his shoulders. He gripped her gorgeous round hips.

By the time he saw her head tilt back, her lips part and felt her fingernails dig into his skin, he knew he couldn't hold back when she came this time. He let the force of her orgasm pull him over the edge. They held on to each other tight while the waves of pleasure crashed over them, leaving them wrung out and panting.

Breathless.

Miles found a corner of the folded duvet at the foot of the bed and hauled it around them as he laid them both back down. They were still sideways on the mattress, but it didn't matter. He couldn't move until the world righted. For now, he tucked her close to him, kissing the top of her head, needing her next to him.

He breathed in the scent of her skin and sex, the passion haze behind his eyelids slowly clearing. He'd wanted to make her feel good, and he was pretty sure he'd accomplished that much. What he hadn't counted on was the way being with her had called forth more than a heady release. He'd damned near forgotten his name.

And even worse? After today, he was pretty sure he'd never be able to dig this woman out of his system.

Chiara awoke some hours later, when moonlight filtered through a high transom window over the French doors in the master suite. Even now, Miles's hand rested on her hip as he slept beside her, in just the same position as they'd fallen asleep, her back to his front.

For a moment, she debated making them something to eat since they'd never had dinner, but her body was still too sated sexually to demand any other sustenance. What a decadent pleasure to awake next to this man in her bed.

And yet, no matter how fulfilled her body, her brain already stirred restlessly. After fourteen years, she now knew what had happened to Zach Eldridge. Or at least, she seemed to know as much as Miles did. Miles had insisted he wasn't sure—that none of his friends were sure—whether or not Zach had jumped to end his life or if he'd jumped in a moment of reckless thrill seeking.

Maybe it didn't matter.

But what if it did? What if one of the Mesa Falls Ranch owners knew more about Zach's motives or mindset than they let on? Was one of them more morally responsible than the others for not stopping Zach's trek up to the top of those cliffs in the first place? Was one of them responsible for Zach's death?

She burrowed deeper into her down pillow, trying to shut out the thoughts. If she didn't get some sleep, she wouldn't be able to solve the mystery. Yet her brain kept reminding her that someone knew she was looking into Zach's death, and whoever it was felt threatened enough by her search that he— or she—had tried blackmailing her into giving up.

"Everything okay?" the warm, sleep-roughened voice behind her asked.

A shiver went through her as Miles stroked his palm along her bare hip under the covers. What might it have been like to meet him under different circumstances? Would she have been able to simply relax and enjoy the incredible chemistry?

"Just thinking about Zach. Trying to reconcile the things you told me with my own understanding of him." That was true enough, even if she had bigger concerns, too. Absently, she traced the piping on the white cotton pillowcase.

Propping himself on his elbow, he said, "If he had an affair with a teacher and she ended up pregnant, it definitely accounts for why he was stressed that weekend. She could have gone to prison for being with him, too, which would have provided another level of stress."

His other hand remained on her hip, his fingers tracing idle patterns that gave her goose bumps.

"She put him in a position no seventeen-year-old should ever be in. Who's to say how he felt about her that weekend? He could have been stressed be- cause she ended things with him. Or because someone found out their secret." She tried to envision what would drive Zach to total despair or to feel reckless enough to make that unwise jump. "Then again, maybe he was stressed because she wanted him to commit to her."

Miles's hand stilled. "What nineteen-year-old woman would want to play house with a seventeen-year-old kid?"

"The same woman who would have had an affair with a student in the first place." Even fourteen years later, she felt angry at the woman for taking advantage of someone she should have been protecting. No matter how much more mature Zach seemed than the other students around him, he was still a kid.

"I should check my phone." Rolling away from her, Miles withdrew his hand from under her body to reach for his device on the nightstand. "I might have heard back from the PI about the stakeout around Nicole Cruz's house."

Instantly alert, Chiara sat up in the bed, dragging a sheet with her. The room was still dark except for the moonlight in the transom window, so Chiara flicked the remote button to turn on the gas fireplace. Flames appeared with a soft whoosh while Miles turned on his phone then scrolled through various screens, his muscles lit by the orange glow.

When his finger stopped swiping, she watched his expression as his blue eyes moved back and forth. Tension threaded through his body. She could see it in his jaw and compressed lips.

"What is it? Did they find her?"

For a moment, when he looked up at her blankly, she wondered if he would go back to shutting her out of news about Zach. Or news about this woman— whether or not she had a direct tie to Zach.

But then his expression cleared, and he nodded.

"According to Desmond's note, Nicole Cruz won't return to Mesa Falls with our private investigator until all the ranch owners submit DNA for paternity testing." His voice was flat. His expression inscrutable. "She's agreed to submit a sample from her sister's son."

"That's good news, right?" she asked, feeling a hunch the child wouldn't be linked to any of them. Her gut told her the mystery boy was Zach's son. "And in the meantime, maybe your detective can see if there's a link between Nicole Cruz and the teacher—Lana Allen. Were they really sisters?"

Miles's fingers hovered over his phone screen. "It would be good to have a concrete lead to give him." He hesitated. "Are you comfortable with me sharing what you told me?"

The fact that he would ask her first said a lot about his ability to be loyal. To keep a confidence. He'd certainly maintained secrecy for Zach's sake for a long, long time. The realization comforted her now that she more clearly understood his reluctance to reveal the truth.

"Would you be sharing the information directly with the investigator, or are you asking for permission to communicate it with all your partners?" She understood that Miles trusted his friends, but her first loyalty had to be to Zach.

A veil of coolness dropped over Miles's features as a chill crept into his voice. "Until now, my partners and I have pooled our knowledge."

She waited for him to elaborate, but he didn't.

She needed to tread carefully, not wanting to alienate him now that he'd finally brought her into his confidence. And yet her feelings for him—her fear of losing him—threatened her objectivity. Hugging the sheet tighter to her chest, she felt goose bumps along her arms. If only it was the room getting cooler and not Miles's mood casting a chill. She weighed how to respond.

"I know you trust your friends." She couldn't help it if she didn't. "But you have to admit that the last time you communicated my interest in Zach to that group, the threats against me came very quickly afterward."

If she'd thought his face was cool before, his blue gaze went glacial now.

"Coincidence," he returned sharply. "I'm not in the habit of keeping secrets from the men I trust most."

A pain shot through her as she realized that the last few hours with Miles hadn't shifted his opinion of her or brought them closer together. If anything, she felt further apart from him than ever. The hurt made her lash out, a safer reaction than revealing vulnerability.

"You realize my entire livelihood rests in the balance?" She couldn't help but draw a second blanket over her shoulders like armor, a barrier, feeling the need to shore up her defenses that had dissolved too fast where he was concerned. "And possibly my safety?"

She thought she spied a thaw in his frosty gaze. He set his phone aside and palmed her shoulder, his fingers a warm, welcome weight.

"I've already told you that I will do everything in my power to keep you safe." The rasp in his voice reminded her of other conversations, other confidences he'd shared with her. She wanted to believe in him.

"I want to find out what drove Zach over that cliff as much as anyone." She swallowed back her anxiety and hoped she wasn't making a huge mistake. "If you think it's best to share what I told you with his other friends in addition to the PI, then you're welcome to tell them what I knew about Zach and the teacher—Miss Allen."

Miles's gaze held hers for a moment before he gave a nod and picked up his phone again to type a text. For a long time afterward, Chiara couldn't help but think his expression showed the same uneasiness she felt inside. But once Miles hit the send button, she knew it was too late to turn back from the course they'd already set.

Eleven

Snow blanketed the Tahoe vacation villa, the world of white momentarily distracting Miles from the tension hanging over his head ever since he'd shared Chiara's insights about Zach with his friends two days ago. A storm had taken the power out the day before, giving them a grace period to watch the weather blow in, make love in every room of that huge villa and not think about their time together coming to an end as they got closer to learning the truth about Zach's death.

Miles had continued to shove his concerns to the back burner this morning, managing to talk Chiara into taking a walk through the woods with him after breakfast. They'd ridden a snowmobile to the casino the day before to retrieve some clothes from his suite.

Now, he held her gloved hand in his as they trudged between sugar pines and white fir trees, the accumulation up to their knees in most places. A dusting clung to her jeans and the fringe of her long red wool jacket. Her cheeks were flushed from the cold and the effort of forging a path through the drifts. Her dark hair was braided in a long tail over one shoulder, a white knitted beanie framing her face as she smiled up at a red-tailed hawk who screeched down at them with its distinctive cry.

For a moment, he saw a different side of her. With no makeup and no fans surrounding her, no couture gown or A-list celebrities clamoring for a photo with her, Chiara looked like a woman who might enjoy the same kind of quiet life he did.

But he knew that was only an illusion. She circulated in a glamorous world of nightlife and parties, far from the ranch where he spent his time.

"I'm glad we got out of the house." She leaned against the rough bark of a Jeffrey pine as they reached an overlook of the lake, where the water reflected the dull gray of the snow clouds. "While having a snow day was fun yesterday, it only delayed the stress fallout from visiting the police station and having it posted online. I feel like I'm still waiting for the other shoe to drop."

Miles leaned back against the trunk near her, still holding her hand. The reminder of those things hanging over them still made him uneasy, and he wished he could distract her. How she felt mattered to him more than it should, considering the very lives they led. And how fast she'd be out of his life again.

He knew her time in Tahoe was bound to her search for answers about Zach, which was why Miles hadn't found a way to tell her yet about the DNA test results he'd received from Desmond earlier that morning. All the Mesa Falls owners had been ruled out, as had Alonzo Salazar through DNA provided by his sons. Which meant there was a strong chance Zach was the father. But Miles hadn't shared that yet, knowing damn well Chiara might leave once she knew. The possibility of her going weighed him down like lead, but he was also still worried about her safety after the anonymous threats. But he ignored his own feelings to try to reassure her.

"It's been two days since the photos of us at the police station started appearing online." He'd checked his phone before driving over to the casino for his clothes, wanting to make sure there'd been no backlash from her fans. "Maybe it won't be a big deal."

Below them on the snowy hill, a few kids dragged snow tubes partway up the incline to sled down to the water, even though the conditions seemed too powdery for a good run. A few vacation cabins dotted the coastline, and he guessed they were staying in one of them. Chiara's gaze followed the kids, too, before she looked up at him.

"Maybe not." She didn't sound convinced. "And my social media accounts are still working." She held up her phone with the other hand. "I successfully posted a photo of the snow-covered trees a moment ago."

While he was glad to hear her accounts hadn't been hacked, he was caught off guard by the idea of her posting nature photos to her profile that was full of fashion. And he was grateful to think about something besides the guilt gnawing at him for not confiding in her about the DNA news.

"Just trees?" He gave her a sideways glance, studying her lovely profile.

Her lips pursed in thought. "I've been posting more artistic images." She shifted against the tree trunk so she faced him, her breath huffing between them in a drift of white in the cold air. "Thinking more about Zach this week has made me question how I could have gotten so far afield from the mixed media art that I used to love making."

Regret rose as he remembered how he'd dismissed her work when they'd first met. "I hope it didn't have anything to do with what I said that night about your job. I had no right—"

She shook her head, laying a hand on his arm. "Absolutely not. I know why I launched my brand and created the blog since I couldn't afford art school. But there's nothing stopping me from doing something different now. From reimagining my future."

While the kids on the hill below them laughed

and shouted over their next sled run, Miles shifted toward Chiara, the tree bark scraping his sheepskin jacket as he wondered if she could reimagine a future with him in it. Did he want that? Gazing into her green eyes, he still wrestled with how much they could trust each other. He felt her wariness about his friends. And for his part, he knew she was only here now because of her loyalty to Zach.

So he kept his response carefully focused on her even when he was tempted as hell to ask for more.

"No doubt, you could do anything you wanted now." He brushed a snowflake from her cheek, the feel of her reminding him of all the best highlights from their past two nights together.

Funny that despite seeing stars many times thanks to her, the moments he remembered best were how she'd felt wrapped around him as he fell asleep the last two nights, resulting in the best slumber he'd had in a long time. He'd been totally relaxed, like she was supposed to be right there with him.

She closed her eyes for a moment as he touched her. He'd like to think she relished the feel of him as much he did her. Her long lashes fluttered against her cheeks for a moment before she raised her gaze to meet his again.

"For a long time, I worried that any artistic talent I once had was only because of the inspiration from the year I knew Zach," she confided quietly. "Like I was somehow a fraud without him."

The statement stunned him, coming from someone so obviously talented. "You built your success because of your artistic eye. And hell yes, I know that because I read up on you after we met."

He wasn't about to hide that from her if he could leverage what he'd learned to reassure her. He lifted her chin so she could see his sincerity.

"Thank you." Her gloved fingers wrapped around his wrist where he touched her, the leather creaking softly with the cold. "Oddly, I've been more reassured as I've reconnected with my old sketchbooks. There is a lot more original work in there than I remembered. I think I let Zach's influence magnify in my mind over the years because of the huge hole he left in my life in other ways. I spent at least a year just redrawing old works of his from memory, trying to keep him in my heart."

Tenderness for her loss swamped him. He recognized it. He'd lived it. "I know what you mean. All of us tried to fill the void he left in different ways. Weston took up search and rescue work. Gage disappeared into numbers and investing."

He mused over the way his friends had grown an unbreakable bond, while at the same time venturing decidedly away from the experience they'd shared. Zach's death had brought them together and kept them all isolated at the same time.

"What about you?" Chiara asked as his hand fell from her chin. "What did you do afterward?"

He couldn't help a bitter smile. "I became the

model son. I threw myself into ranching work to help my father and prepare for taking over Rivera Ranch."

"That sounds like a good thing, right?" She tipped her head sideways as if not sure what she was hearing. "Very practical."

"Maybe it was. But it only increased the divide between my brother and me." He hated that time in his life for so many reasons. The fact that it had alienated him from the person who knew him best had been a pain that lasted long after. "I could do no wrong in my parents' eyes after that, and it was the beginning of the end for my relationship with Wes."

Her brows knit in confusion as the snow started falling faster. A flake clung briefly to her eyelash before melting.

"Why would your brother resent your efforts to help your family?" she asked with a clarity he could never muster for the situation.

The fact that she saw his life—him—so clearly had him struggling to maintain his distance. The intimacy of the last two days was threatening to pull him under. Needing a breather, he stirred from where he stood.

"He didn't." Miles shrugged as he straightened, gesturing toward the path back to her villa. "But our parents treated us so differently it got uncomfortable for Wes to even come home for holidays. I hated how they treated him, too, but since I spent every second away from school working on Rivera Ranch, I let that take over my life."

For a few minutes, they shuffled back along the paths they'd made through the deep snow on their way out. He, for one, was grateful for the reprieve from a painful topic. But then again, if there was a chance he would be spending more time with Chiara in the future, he owed her an explanation of his family dynamics.

He held his hand out for her to help her over an icy log in the path.

"It seems like the blame rests on your parents' shoulders. Not yours or Weston's," she observed, jumping down from the log to land beside him with a soft thud of her heavy boots.

The sounds from the sledders retreated as they continued through the woods.

"Maybe so. But then, on one of Wes's rare trips home, we ended up dating the same woman without knowing. That didn't help things." It had been a misguided idea to date Brianna in the first place, but Miles had been on the ranch and isolated for too long. So even though Brianna was a rebel and a risk taker, he'd told himself his life needed more adventure.

He'd gotten far more than he'd bargained for when he'd seen Wes in a lip lock with her at a local bar a few weeks later. That betrayal had burned deep.

"That sounds like her fault. Because you may not have known, but she must have." She scowled as she spoke.

Miles couldn't help a laugh. "I appreciate your defense of me. Thank you."

He could see Chiara's villa ahead through the trees and the snow, and his steps slowed. He wasn't ready to return to the real world yet. Didn't want to know what had happened with Nicole Cruz, or with Chiara's anonymous hacker. He wanted more time with her before he lost her to her work and her world where he didn't belong.

Chiara slowed, too, coming to a halt beside him. They still held hands. And for some reason stepping out of the trees felt like it was bringing them that much closer to the end of their time together.

"I like you, Miles," she admitted, dropping her forehead to rest on his shoulder as if she didn't want to return to the real world yet, either. "In case you haven't guessed."

Her simple words plucked at something inside him. Made him want to take a chance again for the first time in a long time. Or confide in her, at the very least. But long-ingrained habit kept him silent about the deeper things he was feeling. Instead, he focused on the way they connected best.

"I like you a whole lot, too," he growled, winding an arm around her waist to press her more tightly to him. "I'll remind you how much if you take me home with you."

She lifted her eyes to his, and for the briefest of seconds, he thought he saw her hesitate. But then her lids fell shut and she grazed her lips over his, meeting his kiss with a sexy sigh and more than a little heat.

* * *

Chiara was half dazed by the time Miles broke the kiss. Heat rose inside her despite the snow, her body responding to everything about him. His scent. His touch. His wicked, wonderful tongue.

Heartbeat skipping, she gladly followed him as he led her back toward the huge stone-and-wood structure, her thoughts racing ahead to where they'd take the next kiss. Her bed? The sauna? In front of the massive fireplace? Sensual thoughts helped keep her worries at bay after the way Miles seemed to pull back from her earlier. Or had that been her imagination?

Sometimes she sensed that he avoided real conversation in favor of touching and kissing. But when his every touch and kiss set her aflame, could she really argue? She'd let her guard down around him in a big way, showing him a side of herself that felt new. Vulnerable. Raw.

Breathless with anticipation, she tripped into the side door behind him, peeling off her snowy boots on the mat. Her hat and gloves followed. He shook off his coat and boots before stripping off her jacket and hanging it on an antique rack for her. He didn't wait to fold her in his arms and kiss her again. He gripped her hips, steadying her as he sealed their bodies together. Heat scrambled her thoughts again, her fingers tunneling impatiently under his cashmere sweater where she warmed them against his back before walking them around to his front, tucking them in the waistband of his jeans.

The ragged sound in his throat expressed the same need she felt, and he pulled away long enough to grip her by the hand and guide her across the polished planked floor toward the stairs.

Her feet were on the first wide step of the formal divided staircase when a knock sounded on the back door.

Miles stopped. His blue gaze swung around to look at her.

Her belly tightened.

"Maybe it's just Jules checking to see how we're faring after the storm." At least, she hoped that was all it was.

Still, her feet didn't move until the knock sounded again. More urgently.

"We'd better check," Miles muttered, frustration punctuating every word. He kept holding her hand as he walked with her through the kitchen.

She sensed the tension in him—something about the way he held himself. Or maybe the way he looked like he was grinding his teeth. But she guessed that was the same sexual frustration she was feeling right now.

Still, her nerves wound tight as she padded through the room in her socks. Through a side window, she could see Jules and Stefan—together—on the back step. Vaguely, she felt Miles give her hand a reassuring squeeze before she pulled open the door.

"What's up?" she started to ask, only to have Jules thrust her phone under Chiara's nose as she stepped into the kitchen, Stefan right behind her.

Miles closed the door.

"Your page is down." Jules's face was white, her expression grim as she waggled the phone in front of Chiara with more emphasis. "We've been hacked."

She could have sworn the floor dropped out from under her feet. Miles's arm wrapped around her. Steadying her.

Chiara stared at Jules's device, afraid to look. Closing her eyes for a moment, she took a deep breath before she accepted the phone. Then, sinking onto the closest counter stool, she tapped the screen back to life.

Miles peered over her shoulder, his warmth not giving her the usual comfort as a shiver racked her. His hand rubbed over her back while her eyes focused on what she was seeing.

Oddly, the image at the top of her profile page— her home screen—was of Miles. Only he wasn't alone. It was a shot of him with his face pressed cheek to cheek with a gorgeous woman—a brown-eyed beauty with dark curling hair and a mischievous smile. A banner inserted across the image read, "Kara Marsh, you'll always be second best."

Miles might have said something in her ear, but she couldn't focus on his words. If she'd thought the floor had shifted out from under her feet before, now her stomach joined the free fall. As images went, it wasn't particularly damaging to her career.

Simply to her heart.

Because the look on Miles's face in that photo was one she'd never seen before. Pressed against that ethereally gorgeous creature, Miles appeared happier than he'd ever been with Chiara. In this image, his blue eyes were unguarded. Joyous. In love.

And that hurt more than anything. In the woods this morning, when she'd tentatively tested out his feelings with a confession that she liked him—not that it was a huge overture, but still, she'd tried— he'd responded with sizzle. Not emotions.

Jules crouched down into her line of vision, making Chiara realize she'd been silent too long. With an effort, she tried to recover herself, knowing full well her hurt must have been etched all over her face in those first moments when she'd seen the picture.

"It could be worse," she managed to say, sliding the phone across the granite countertop to Jules, avoiding pieces from a jigsaw puzzle she'd worked on for a little while with Miles during the snowstorm. "That's hardly a damning shot."

"I agree," Jules said softly, her tone a careful blend of professionalism and caution. "But the banner— coupled with the fact that you were recently photographed with Miles—creates the impression that either Miles or his—" she hesitated, shooting a quick glance at Miles "—um, former girlfriend were the ones to hijack your social media properties. This same image is on your personal blog, too. I'm worried your fans will be defensive of you—"

"I'm sure we'll get it cleared up soon." She wasn't sure of any such thing as she picked up one of the puzzle pieces and traced the tabs and slots. But the need to confront Miles privately was too strong for her to think about her career. Or whatever else Jules was saying. "Could you give us a minute, Jules? And I'll come over to help you figure out our next steps in a little while?"

Her heartbeat pounded too loudly for her to even be sure what Jules said on her way out. But her friend took Stefan by the arm—even though her bodyguard looked doubtfully from Miles to Chiara and back again—and tugged him out the villa's back door.

Leaving her and Miles alone.

He put his hands on her shoulders, gently swiveling her on the counter stool so that she faced him.

"Are you all right?" He lowered himself into the seat next to her, perching on the edge of the leather cushion. "Would you like me to get you something to drink? You don't look well."

"I'm fine." That wasn't true, but a drink wouldn't help the tumultuous feelings inside her. The hurt deeper than she had a right to feel over a man she'd vowed could only be a fling.

"You don't look fine." His blue eyes were full of concern. Though, she reminded herself, not love. "You can't think for a second I had anything to do with posting that."

"Of course not." That hadn't even occurred to her. She hadn't roused the energy to think about who was behind the post because she was too busy having her heart stepped on. Too consumed with feelings she'd assured herself she wasn't going to develop for this man. But judging by the jealousy and hurt gnawing away at her insides, she couldn't deny she'd been harboring plenty of emotions for this man.

Still, she needed to pull herself together.

"For what it's worth, that's obviously not a recent photo," Miles offered, his hands trailing down her arms to her hands where he found the puzzle piece she was still holding. He set it back on the counter. "I'm not sure where someone would have gotten ahold of it, but—"

"Social media," she supplied, thinking she really needed to get back online and start scouring her pages to see what was happening. Jules had to be wondering why Chiara had only wanted to talk to Miles. "It looks like a selfie. My guess is your old girlfriend has it stored on one of her profiles."

"Makes sense." He nodded, straightening, his touch falling away from her. "But I was going to say that I haven't seen Brianna Billings in years, so I'm sure she wouldn't be sending you anonymous threats."

Not wanting to discuss the woman in the photo, or the feelings it stirred, Chiara stared out the window behind Miles's head and watched the snowfall as she turned the conversation in another direction.

"So if we rule out you and your ex for suspects in hacking the page," she continued, knowing she sounded stiff. Brusque. "Who else should we look at? I'll call the police again, of course, but they'll ask us who we think might be responsible. And personally, I think it's got to be one of your partners at Mesa Falls. One of Zach's former friends."

"No." He shook his head resolutely and stood, then walked over to the double refrigerator doors and pulled out a bottle of water. He set it on the island before retrieving two glasses. "It can't be."

She didn't appreciate how quickly he wrote off her idea. Especially when her feelings were already stirred up disproportionately at seeing a different side of Miles in that photo. She felt Miles pulling away. Sensed it was all plummeting downhill between them, but she didn't have a clue how to stop things from going off the rails.

"Who else would be tracking my efforts to find out what happened to Zach, and would know about your past, too?" she asked him sharply. "I'm not the common denominator in that equation. It's the Mesa Falls group."

"It's someone trying to scare you away from looking into Zach's past. Maybe Nicole Cruz?" he mused aloud as he filled the two glasses of water. Although as soon as he said it, he glanced up at her, and she could have sworn she saw a shadow cross through his eyes.

Then again, she was feeling prickly. She tried

to let go of the hurt feelings while he returned the water bottle to the stainless steel refrigerator. Frustration and hurt were going to help her get to the bottom of this.

"It could be whoever fathered the mystery child," she pressed, wondering about the DNA evidence. "Once we know who the father is—"

"It's none of us," Miles answered with a slow shake of his head. He set a glass of water in front of her as he returned to the seat beside her.

His answer sounded certain. As if he knew it for a fact. But she guessed that was just his way of willing it to be the truth.

"We'll only know that for sure once the test results come in," she reminded him before taking a sip of her drink.

"They already have. All of the Mesa Falls partners have been cleared of paternity, along with Alonzo Salazar, courtesy of DNA provided by his sons." Miles's fingers tightened around his glass.

Surprised, Chiara set hers back down with a thud, sloshing some over the rim.

"How long have you known?" she asked, her nerve endings tingling belatedly with uneasiness.

"Desmond texted me early this morning."

"And just when were you going to tell me?" She knew logically that not much time had passed. But she'd been waiting half of a lifetime for answers about Zach. And damn it, she'd spent her whole life being in the dark because of other people's secrets.

Her family's. Zach's friends'. Even, she had to admit, Zach's.

Indignation burned. Her heart pounded faster, her body recognizing the physical symptoms of betrayal. Of secrets hidden.

"Soon," Miles started vaguely, not meeting her eyes. "I just didn't want—"

"You know what? It doesn't matter what you did or didn't want." She stood up in a hurry, needing to put distance between herself and this man who'd slid past her defenses without her knowing. She didn't have the resources to argue with him when her heart hurt, and she'd be damned if she'd let him crush more of the feelings she'd never meant to have for him.

She needed to get her coat so she could go talk to Jules and focus on her career instead of a man who would never trust her. More than that, she needed to get out of the same town as him. Out of the same state.

There was no reason to linger here any longer. The time had come to return home, back to her own life in Los Angeles.

"Chiara, wait." Miles cut her off, inserting himself in her path, though he didn't touch her.

"I can't do secrets, Miles," she said tightly, betrayal stinging. And disillusionment. And anger at herself. "I'm sure that sounds hypocritical after the way I searched your computer that night—"

"It doesn't." He looked so damned good in his

jeans and soft gray sweater, his jaw bristly and un-shaven. "I know trust comes hard for you."

"For you, too, it seems." She folded her arms to keep herself from touching him. If only the want could be so easily held at bay.

"Yes. For me, too," he acknowledged.

She waited for a long moment. Waited. And heaven help her, even hoped. Just a little. But he said nothing more.

Tears burning her eyes, she sidestepped him to reach for her coat.

"I'm going to be working the rest of the day," she informed him, holding herself very straight in an ef-fort to keep herself together. Her heart ached. "I'll head back to LA tomorrow. But for tonight, I think it would be best if you weren't here when I return."

Miles didn't argue. He only nodded. He didn't even bother to fight for her.

Once she had her boots and coat on, she shoved through the door and stepped out into the snow. Some wistful part of her thought she heard a softly spoken, "Don't go" from behind her. But she knew it was just the foolish wish of a heart broken before she'd even realized she'd fallen in love.

Twelve

Three days later, gritty-eyed despite rising late, Miles prowled Desmond's casino floor at noon. Navigating the path to Desmond's office through a maze of roulette wheels, blackjack tables and slot machines, he cursed the marketing wisdom that demanded casino guests walk through the games every time they wanted to access hotel amenities.

No doubt the setup netted Desmond big profits, but the last thing Miles wanted to see after Chiara's defection was a tower of lights blinking "jackpot!" accompanied by a chorus of electronic enthusiasm. A herd of touristy-looking players gathered around the machine to celebrate their good fortune, while Miles suspected he'd never feel lucky again.

Not after losing the most incredible woman he'd ever met just two weeks after finding her. He'd surely set a record for squandering everything in so little time.

He hadn't been able to sleep for thinking about the expression on her face when she'd discovered he hadn't told her about the DNA test results. He'd known—absolutely known—that she would be hurt by that given the trust issues she'd freely admitted. And yet he'd withheld it anyhow, unwilling to share the news that would send her out of his life.

So instead of letting her choose when she should return to her California home once she'd found out all she could about Zach, he'd selfishly clung to the information in the hope of stretching out their time together. And for his selfishness, he'd hurt her. Sure, he'd like to think he would have told her that afternoon. He couldn't possibly have gone to bed by her side that night without sharing the news. But it didn't matter how long he'd kept that secret.

What mattered was that she'd told him how hard it was for her to trust. Something he—of all people—understood only too well. Yeah, he recognized the pain he'd caused when he'd crossed the one line she'd drawn with him about keeping secrets.

When he finally reached the locked door of the back room, a uniformed casino employee entered a code and admitted him. At least the maze of halls here was quiet. The corridors with their unadorned light gray walls led to a variety of offices and maintenance rooms. Miles bypassed all of them until he reached stately double doors in the back.

Another uniformed guard stood outside them. This one rapped his knuckles twice on the oak barrier before admitting Miles.

A stunning view of Lake Tahoe dominated one side of the owner's work suite, with glass walls separating a private office, small conference room and a more intimate meeting space. All were spare and modern in shades of gray and white, with industrial touches like stainless steel work lamps and hammered metal artwork. Desmond sat on a low sofa in front of the windows overlooking Lake Tahoe in the more casual meeting space.

Sunlight reflecting off the water burned right into Miles's eyes until he moved closer to the window, the angle of built-in blinds effectively shading the glare as he reached his friend. Dressed in a sharp gray suit and white collared shirt with no tie, Desmond drank a cup of espresso as he read an honest-to-God newspaper—no electronic devices in sight. The guy had an easy luxury about him that belied a packed professional life.

As far as Miles knew, he did nothing but work 24/7, the same way Gage Striker had when he'd been an investment banker. Gage's wealth had convinced him to start taking it easier as an angel investor the last couple of years, but Desmond still burned the candle at both ends, working constantly.

"Look what the cat dragged in," Desmond greeted

him, folding his paper and setting it on a low glass table in front of him. With his posh manners and charm, Desmond looked every inch the worldly sophisticate. And it wasn't just an act, either, as he held dual citizenship in the United States and the UK thanks to a Brit mother.

But Miles remembered him from darker days, when Desmond's father had been a ham-fisted brute, teaching his son to be quick with a punch out of necessity, to protect himself and his mother. It was a skill set Desmond hid well, but Miles knew that a lot of his work efforts still benefited battered women and kids. And he'd channeled his own grief about Zach into something positive, whereas Miles still felt like the old wounds just ate away at his insides. What did he have to show for the past beyond Rivera Ranch? All his toil had gone into the family property. And he hadn't really done anything altruistic.

"I only came to let you know I'm returning to Mesa Falls." Miles dropped onto a leather chair near the sofa, eager to leave the place where his brief relationship with Chiara had imploded. "I'm meeting the pilot this afternoon."

"Coffee?" Desmond offered as he picked up a black espresso cup.

Miles shook his head, knowing caffeine wouldn't make a dent in the wrung-out feeling plaguing his head. He'd barely slept last night for thinking about Chiara's parting words that had been so polite and still so damned cutting.

I think it would be best if you weren't here when I return.

"It's just as well you came in." Desmond set aside his empty cup and leaned back into the sofa cushions. "I was going to message you anyhow to let you know you don't need to return to Mesa Falls."

Miles frowned as he rubbed his eyes to take away some of the gritty feeling. "What do you mean? Someone's got to oversee things."

"Nicole Cruz is flying to Montana tonight," Desmond informed him, brushing some invisible item from the perfectly clean cushion by his thigh. "I assured her I would be there to meet her. Them."

Miles edged forward in his seat, trying to follow.

"You want to be there to meet the guardian of the kid who's most likely Zach's son?" he clarified, knowing something was off about the way Desmond was talking about her.

Was it suspicion?

He'd like to think they were all suspicious of her, though. This seemed like something different.

"I've been her only point of contact so far," Desmond explained, giving up on the invisible dust. He gave Miles a level gaze. "The only one of us she's communicated with. We can't afford to scare her off when it took us this long to find her."

"Right. Agreed." Miles nodded, needing to rouse himself out of his own misery to focus on their latest discovery about Zach. "If Matthew is Zach's son, we don't want to lose our chance of being a part of his life."

Regret stung as he considered how much Chiara would want to meet the boy. He didn't want to stand in her way, especially when they might not have come this far figuring out Zach's secrets without her help.

Desmond's phone vibrated, and he picked it up briefly.

"I've asked the PI to back off investigating Nicole and Matthew," Desmond continued as he read something and then set the device back on the table. Sun glinted off the sleek black case.

"Why?" Miles picked up his own phone, checking for the thousandth time if there were any developments on who had targeted Chiara's sites. Or, if he was honest, to see if she had messaged him. Disappointment to find nothing stung all over again.

He missed her more than if she'd been out of his life for years and not days. He'd only stuck around Lake Tahoe this long in hopes he'd be able to help the local police, or maybe in the hope she'd return to town to see Astrid. Or him.

But there was only a group message from Alec telling any of the Mesa Falls partners still on site at the casino to meet him at Desmond's office as soon as possible. Miles wondered what that was about.

"Nicole has been dodging our investigators to protect Matthew for weeks. She's exhausted and mistrustful. She asked me to 'call off the dogs' if she agreed to return to Montana, and I have given her my word that I would." Desmond straightened in his seat, appearing ready to move on as he checked his watch. "And, actually, I have a lot to do today to prepare my staff for my absence. Alec agreed to watch over things here, but he's late."

As he spoke, however, a knock sounded at the outer double doors before they opened, and Alec appeared.

Miles only had a second to take in his friend's disheveled clothes that looked slept in—a wrinkled jacket and T-shirt and rumpled jeans. His hair stood up in a few directions, and his face had a look of grim determination as he wound through the office suite to the glassed-in room where Desmond and Miles sat.

"Sorry I'm late." Alec juggled a foam coffee cup in his hand as he plowed through the last door. "I've been at the police station giving my statement. They arrested my personal assistant, Vivian, for threatening Chiara Campagna."

"You're kidding." Miles tensed, half rising to his feet. Then, realizing the woman in question was already in custody, he lowered himself into the chair again. "How did they find out?"

Miles had checked with the local police just the night before but hadn't learned anything other than that they were still looking into the complaint Chiara filed after the second incident.

Alec lowered himself into the chair opposite

Miles at the other end of the coffee table. He set his coffee cup on a marble coaster.

"Apparently it wasn't tough to track her once they got a cybercrimes expert to look into it. Vivian and I were working late last night when she got a call from the police asking her to come in so they could ask her some questions." Alec shrugged and then swiped his hand through the hair that was already standing straight up. "I drove her over there, never thinking they already had evidence on her. They arrested her shortly afterward."

"Does Chiara know?" Miles wanted to call her. Check on her. Let her know that the police had done their job.

Hell. What he really wanted was to fold her into his arms.

But holding her wasn't his right anymore.

"I'm not sure if they've contacted her yet." Alec retrieved his coffee cup, a thick silver band around his middle finger catching the light and refracting it all over the room. "I'm still trying to process the news myself."

Before Miles could ask more about it, a knock sounded again on the outer door, and his brother, Weston, ambled in wearing jeans and a T-shirt. With his too-long hair and hazel eyes, he and Miles couldn't be less alike.

"What's up? April and I were going to hit the slopes today. Conditions are incredible." He stopped himself as he looked around at his friends. "What happened?"

As he sank to a seat on the other end of the couch from Desmond, Alec repeated the news about Vivian before adding, "I had no idea Vivian was imagining we had a much deeper relationship than we do, but sometime in the last few years she started crossing the line as my assistant to make sure things went my way—bribing contacts into taking meetings with me, padding the numbers on our financial statements to make the gaming company look stronger for investors, a whole bunch of stuff unrelated to what happened with Chiara."

Miles recalled meeting Vivian lurking outside the high-roller suite that day after the meeting of the Mesa Falls partners. "So why would she hassle Chiara?"

"I guess she intercepted a text on my phone about Chiara's interest in Zach." Alec glanced upward, as if trying to gather his thoughts, or maybe to remember something. "Vivian never liked her. She was a student at Brookfield, too, and I was with her that day at Dowdon that Kara—Chiara—came to school to talk to Miles and Gage."

Miles remembered Alec saying he'd been with a girl under the bleachers that day. Still, fourteen years seemed like a long time to hold a grudge against Chiara. Once again his protective instincts kicked into gear. If he couldn't be with Chiara or make her happy, he owed it to her to at least keep her safe.

Which meant getting full disclosure on everything related to Zach's death.

Desmond spoke before Miles had a chance to ask about that.

"So Vivian must have known about Zach if you've been friends that long." Desmond seemed to put the pieces together faster, but maybe it was easier to have more clarity on the situation than Miles, who'd lost objectivity where Chiara was concerned a long time ago. "Maybe she figured it was somehow helping you to keep Chiara from asking too many questions."

Weston whistled softly under his breath. "She sounds like a piece of work."

Alec bristled. "She's smart as hell, actually. Just highly unethical."

The conversation continued, but Miles couldn't focus on it with the urge to see Chiara, to make sure she knew that her hacker was in custody, so strong. He wanted to share the news with her, to give her this much even though he'd failed their fledgling relationship.

"Why did she feel the need to post a picture of me with an old girlfriend on Chiara's page?" he found himself asking, curious not so much for himself, but for Chiara's sake. He'd known that image had bothered her.

And if he was able to see her again—or even just speak to her—he wanted to share answers with her. Answers he owed her after the way he'd withheld information from her before.

Alec took another drink of his coffee before responding. "I wondered about that, too. I guess Vivian was upset about a photo of me with Chiara from that night at your party, Miles. Then, when she saw the pictures of you at the police station with Chiara—looking like a couple—she figured the best way to hurt Chiara would be with an image of you and someone else."

Miles remembered the jealousy that had gone through him when he saw Alec's hand on the small of Chiara's back that night, touching her bare skin through the cutout of her silver gown.

Weston spoke up. "For a smart woman, she definitely made some stupid mistakes. But lucky for us, right? Because now she's behind bars." He stood as if to leave. "I've got to get back to April to meet the car taking us to the mountain."

Miles rose as well, edgy to be out of Tahoe. Now that he'd been relieved of his duties at Mesa Falls, he was free to use the afternoon's flight to see Chiara. To share what he'd learned, at least. "Desmond, if you've got things covered at Mesa Falls, I'm going to head back home."

"You're returning to Rivera Ranch?" Desmond stood and walked to the door with them, though his question was for Miles.

"Eventually." Miles could only think about one destination today, however. "I need to make a stop in Los Angeles first."

After a quick exchange of pleasantries, Miles and Weston left the owner's suite together.

"Los Angeles?" Weston wasted no time in posing the question.

Slowing his step in the long, empty corridor between the casino floor and the offices, Miles couldn't deny the rare impulse to unburden himself. His brother, after all, owed him a listening ear after the way Miles had helped him patch up his relationship with April Stephens, the woman Wes loved beyond reason.

"I messed up with Chiara," he admitted, done with trying to label what happened as anything other than his fault. "I was selfish. Stupid. Shortsighted—"

Weston halted in the middle of the echoing hall, clamping a hand on Miles's shoulder. "What happened?"

Miles explained the way he'd withheld the news about the DNA evidence to give himself more time with her, to try to think of a way to make her stay, even though he'd known about her past and the way her own family had kept secrets from her. Even though she'd told him how hard it was for her to trust. When he finished, Weston looked thoughtful.

"You remember when I screwed up with April, you told me that I needed to be the one to take a risk. To put myself on the line?"

"Yes." Miles remembered that conversation. Of course, taking chances was like breathing to his brother, so it hadn't seemed like too much to ask of him to be the one to tell April he loved her. "I also told you that not everyone can be such a romantic."

Miles knew himself too well. He had two feet on the ground at all times. He was a practical man. Salt of the earth. A rancher. He didn't jump first and ask questions later. That had always been Wes's role. But maybe it was time to take a page from his brother's book, to step up and take a risk when the moment called for it. His gut burned to think he hadn't already done so.

"News flash. What you're feeling doesn't have a thing to do with romance. It has everything to do with love, and you're going to lose it, without question, if you can't get your head on straight and see that." Weston's expression was dire.

Grave.

And Miles wasn't too proud to admit it scared the hell of out of him. Especially if what he'd walked away from was love. But by the way the word encapsulated every single aspect of his feelings for Chiara, he knew Weston was right.

"You think I already blew it for good?" He wondered how fast his plane could get to LA.

"It's been three days and you haven't even called? Haven't gone there to tell her how wrong you were?" Weston shook his head. "Why didn't you call me sooner to help you figure this out? I owed you, man. Maybe, with more time, I could have—"

Miles cut his brother off, panic welling up in his chest.

"I've got a plane to catch." He didn't wait to hear any more about how much he'd screwed up. If time was of the essence, he wasn't wasting another second of it to see Chiara and tell her how he felt about her.

That he loved her.

Thirteen

Seated in a low, rolled-arm chair close to her balcony, Chiara sniffed a small vial of fragrance, knowing she'd have a headache soon if she kept testing the samples from her perfumer. Although maybe the impending headache had more to do with all the tears she'd shed for Miles this week. Still, she needed the distraction from her hurt, so she sniffed the floral fumes again, trying to pinpoint what she didn't like about the scent.

The setting sun smudged the western sky with lavender and pink as lights glowed in the valley below her Hollywood Hills home. The glass wall was retracted between her living room and the balcony so that the night air circulated around the seating area where she tested the samples. She'd adored this property once, so modern and elegant, but it felt incredibly lonely to her since she'd returned to it earlier in the week. As for the fragrance vial in her hand, the hint of honeysuckle—so pleasing in nature—was too heavy in the mixture. She handed it back to Mrs. Santor, her housekeeper. In addition to her regular duties, she was giving her input on developing a signature fragrance for Chiara's brand.

"I didn't like that one, either," Mrs. Santor said from the seat beside her, packing away the vial in a kit Chiara had received from a perfumer. "You should call it a night, honey. You look spent."

Amy Santor was Jules's mother and a former next-door neighbor in Chiara's old life. Mrs. Santor had cleaned houses all her life, and when Chiara's business had taken off, she would have gladly given Mrs. Santor any job she wanted in her company to repay her for kindnesses she'd shown Chiara in her youth. But Jules's mom insisted that she enjoyed keeping house, and Chiara felt fortunate to have a maternal figure in her home a few times a week.

"I shouldn't be. It's still early." She checked her watch, irritated with herself for not being more focused.

She'd given Jules a much-needed night off but hadn't taken one herself, preferring to lose herself in work ever since the heartbreak of leaving Lake Tahoe.

She'd heard from a detective today about arresting the woman who'd hijacked her social media, so it should have felt like she had closure. But that conversation had only made her realize how much more losing Miles had hurt her than any damage a hacker could wreak.

At any rate, she'd *tried* to lose herself in work since that had always been her escape. Her purpose. Her calling. She'd built it up in spite of the grief she'd had for Zach, trusting the job to keep her grounded. But it didn't provide a refuge for her now.

"I'll make you some tea before I go," Mrs. Santor continued, putting away the paperwork from the fragrance kit. "I know you don't want to talk about whatever happened on your travels, but trust me when I tell you that you need to take care of yourself."

And with a gentle squeeze to Chiara's shoulder, Mrs. Santor started the kettle to boil in the kitchen while Chiara tried to pull herself together. Maybe she should have confided in her longtime friend. She hadn't talked to Jules, either, refusing to give the people she loved the chance to comfort her.

For so many years she'd been an island—isolated, independent, and no doubt taking too much pride in the fact. But what good was pride when she felt so empty inside now?

Walking away from Miles was the hardest thing she'd ever done. Second only to the restraint it took every day—every hour—not to call or text him. She wondered if he'd returned to Mesa Falls by now or if he'd gone back to Rivera Ranch. Mostly, she wondered if he ever missed her or regretted the way they'd parted.

A moment later, Mrs. Santor returned with a steaming cup and set it before her. "I'm heading out now, hon. I'll see you Saturday, okay?"

Grateful for the woman's thoughtfulness, Chiara rose and hugged her. "Thank you."

Jules's mother hugged her back with the same warmth she gave her own daughter. "Of course. And don't work too hard."

When Mrs. Santor left, Chiara settled in for the evening. But just as she took a sip of her tea to ward off the loneliness of her empty house, the guard buzzed her phone from the gate downstairs. She picked up her device.

"Ms. Campagna, there's a Miles Rivera to see you."

Everything inside her stilled.

There'd been a time he could have had security toss her out of his home for invading his privacy, but instead, he'd listened to her explanation. For that alone, he deserved an audience now. But more than that, she couldn't resist the chance to see him again. She'd missed him so much.

"You can let him in," she answered, feelings tumbling over each other too fast for her to pick through them.

She'd been thinking about him and wishing she could see him. Now that he was here, was she brave enough to take a chance with him? She didn't want to let Miles go, either. What good did her pride do her if it left her feeling heartbroken and lonely?

Chiara resisted the urge to peek in a mirror, although she may have fluffed her hair a little and smoothed her dress. Who didn't want to look their best in front of the one who got away?

She rose from the seat to stand out on the balcony. Even though she was staring out at the spectacular view with her back to the house, Chiara could tell when Miles was close. The hairs on the back of her neck stood, a shiver of awareness passing over her. She pressed her lips together to ward off the feelings, reminding herself of what had happened to drive them apart.

"I've never seen such a beautiful view." The familiar rasp in his voice warmed her. Stirred her.

Turning on her heel, she faced him as he paced through the living area and out onto the balcony. With his chiseled features and deep blue eyes, his black custom suit that hinted at sculpted muscles and the lightly tanned skin visible at the open collar of his white shirt, he was handsome to behold.

But she remembered so many other things about him that were even more appealing. His thoughtfulness in watching out for her. His insistence she go to the police. His touch.

"Hello to you, too," she greeted him, remembering his fondness for launching right into conversation. "I'm surprised to see you here."

"I wanted to be sure you heard the news." He stepped closer until he leaned against the balcony rail with her. "That your harasser is behind bars."

She shouldn't be disappointed that this practical man would be here for such a pragmatic purpose, yet she couldn't deny she'd hoped for more than that. Should she tell him how much she'd missed him? How many times she'd thought about calling?

Absently, she drummed her fingernails against the polished railing, trying not to notice how close Miles's hands were to hers. "Yes. A detective called me this morning with some questions about Vivian Fraser from our time together at Brookfield. I didn't realize she worked for Alec now."

"Were you aware she was jealous of you?"

"No. I don't remember her well from Brookfield other than recalling she was a popular girl with a lot of friends. Our paths never crossed much, as she favored chess club and science over the art activities that I liked." She'd been stunned to hear that Alec's personal assistant had intercepted his messages and decided to "protect" Zach's memory for him by attempting to scare Chiara away from her search for answers.

But apparently there was a clear digital trail that led to Vivian's personal computer, and she'd admitted as much to the police. The woman was in love with Alec and would do anything to protect him. She'd also done her best to keep other women away from him since they'd had an on-again, off-again relationship dating all the way back to high school. It was sad to think a promising young woman had gotten so caught up in wanting attention from a man that she'd given up her own dreams and identity in an effort to capture his notice.

"I breathed a whole lot easier once I heard the news," Miles said as he looked over the lights spread out below them now that the pink hues of sunset had faded. "I'm sure you did, too."

She couldn't help but glance over at his profile. The strong jaw and chin. The slash of his cheekbone. His lips that could kiss her with infinite tenderness.

"I guess." She spoke quickly once she realized she'd stared too long. "But the whole business with my blog and Vivian were distractions from my real purpose. I really went there to find out about Zach's final days."

She felt more than saw Miles turn toward her now. His eyes looking over her the way she'd studied him just a moment ago. Her heat beat faster as a soft breeze blew her white dress's hem against her legs, the silk teasing her already too-aware skin.

"I know you did, Chiara. And I'm sorry that I got in the way of what you were doing by not sharing what I knew as soon as I knew it." The regret and sincerity in his voice were unmistakable. "You deserved my full help and attention. And so did Zach."

Drawn by his words, she turned toward him now, and they faced one another eye to eye for the first time tonight. He seemed even closer to her now. Near enough to touch.

"I recognize that I probably should have been more understanding. Especially after the way you overlooked me trying to get into your personal files. I crossed a line more than you did." She hadn't forgotten that, and the unfairness of her response compared to his seemed disproportionate. "But I didn't know you when I sneaked into your office. Whereas—"

"The situations were completely different." He shook his head, not letting her finish her sentence. "You had every right to think I might have been a bad friend to Zach or even an enemy. But I knew you had his best interests at heart that day I kept quiet about the DNA. My only defense was that I wanted one more day with you."

Startled, she rewound the words in her mind, barely daring to hope she'd heard him right. "You— what?"

"I knew that once I told you the DNA results you'd have no reason to stay in Tahoe any longer." He touched her forearm. "And our time together had been so incredible, Chiara, I couldn't bear for it to end. I told myself that keeping quiet about it for a few more hours wouldn't hurt. I just wanted—" He shook his head. "It was selfish of me. And I'm sorry."

The admission wasn't at all what she'd expected. "I thought you were keeping secrets to hold me at arm's length. It felt like you didn't want to confide in me."

But this? His reason was far more compelling. And it shot right into the tender recesses of her heart.

"Far from it." A breeze ruffled Miles's hair the way she longed to with her fingers. His hand stroked up her arm to her shoulder. "Talking to you was the highlight of my week. And considering everything else that happened, you have to know how much it meant to me."

She melted inside. Absolutely, positively melted.

"Really?" She'd hoped so, until he'd walked away. But she could see the regret in his eyes now, and it gave her renewed hope.

"Yes, really." He stepped closer to her, one hand sliding around her waist while the other skimmed a few wind-tossed strands of hair from her eyes. "Chiara, I got burned so badly the last time I cared about someone that I planned to be a lot more cautious in the future. I figured if I took my time to build a safe, smart relationship, maybe then I could fall in love."

Her pulse skipped a couple of beats. She blinked up at him, hanging on his words. Trying not to sink into the feeling of his hands on her after so many days of missing him. Missing what they'd shared. Aching for more. For a future.

"I don't understand. Are you suggesting we didn't build a safe relationship?"

"I'm suggesting that whatever my intentions were, they didn't matter at all, because you showed up and we had the most amazing connection I've ever felt with anyone." His hold on her tightened, and she might have stepped a tiny bit closer because the hint of his aftershave lured her.

"I felt that, too," she admitted, remembering how that first night she'd felt like the whole world disappeared except for them. "The amazing connection."

"Right. Good." His lips curved upward just a hint at her words. "Because I came here tonight—why I *really* came here tonight—to tell you that I fell in love with you, Chiara. And if there's any way you can give me another chance, I'm going to do everything in my power to make you fall in love with me, too."

Her heart hitched at his words, which were so much more than she'd dared hope for—but everything she wanted. Touched beyond measure, she couldn't find her voice for a moment. And then, even when she did, she bit her lip, wanting to say the right thing.

"Miles, I knew when we were in the woods that day that I loved you." She laid her hand on his chest beside his jacket lapel, just over his heart. She remembered every minute of their time together. "I didn't even want to go back to the house afterward because it felt like our time together was ending, and I didn't want to lose you."

He wrapped her tight in his arms and kissed her. Slowly. Thoroughly. Until she felt a little weak-kneed from it and the promise it held of even more. When he eased back, she was breathing fast and clinging to him.

"You're not going to lose me. Not now. Not ever."

His blue eyes were dark as midnight, the promise one she'd never forget.

It filled her with certainty about the future. Their future.

"You won't lose me, either," she vowed before freeing a hand to gesture to the view. "Not even if I have to leave all this behind to live on Rivera Ranch with you."

"You don't have to do that." He tipped his forehead to hers. "We can take all the time you want to talk about what makes most sense. Or hell, just what we want. I know you want to go back to art school one day, so we can always look at living close to a good program for you."

No one had ever put her first before, and it felt incredibly special to have Miles do just that. The possibilities expanded.

"You don't need to be at the ranch?" she asked, curious about his life beyond Mesa Falls. She wanted to learn everything about him.

"I've worked hard to make it a successful operation that runs smoothly. I've hired good people to maintain that, so even if I'm not there, the ranch will continue to prosper." He traced her cheek with his fingers, then followed the line of her mouth.

She sucked in a breath, wanting to seal the promise of their future with a kiss, and much, much more. Lifting her eyes to his, she read the same steamy thoughts in his expression.

"I'll be able to weigh the possibilities more after I

show you how much I've missed you," she told him, capturing his thumb between her teeth.

With a growl that thrilled her, he lifted her in his arms and walked her inside the house.

She had a last glimpse of the glittering lights of the Hollywood Hills, but the best view of all was wherever this man was. Miles Rivera, her rancher hero, right here in her arms.

* * * * *

Dynasties: Mesa Falls
Don't miss a single installment!

The Rebel
The Rival
Rule Breaker
Heartbreaker
The Rancher
The Heir

by USA TODAY *bestselling author*
Joanne Rock

Available exclusively
from Harlequin Desire.

"Hopefully everyone will get home safe," she said.

Gabe took in her high cheekbones, the soft roundness of her jaw
and the tilt of her chin. The scent of something subtle but sweet
surrounded her. He forced his eyes away from her and cleared his
throat. "Hopefully," he agreed as he poured a small amount of
champagne into his flute.

"I'll leave you to celebrate," Monica said.

With a polite nod, Gabe took a sip of his drink and set the bottle
at his feet, trying to ignore the reasons why he was so aware of her.
Her scent. Her beauty. Even the gentle night winds shifting her
hair back from her face. Distance was best. Over the past week he
had fought to do just that to help his sudden awareness of her ebb.
Ever since the veil to their desire had been removed, it had been
hard to ignore.

She turned to leave, but moments later a yelp escaped her as
her feet got twisted in the long length of her robe and sent her body
careening toward him as she tripped.

Reacting swiftly, he reached to wrap his arm around her waist
and brace her body up against his to prevent her fall. He let the hand
holding his flute drop to his side. Their faces were just precious

inches apart. When her eyes dropped to his mouth, he released a small gasp. His eyes scanned her face before locking with hers.

He knew just fractions of a second had passed, but right then, with her in his arms and their eyes locked, it felt like an eternity. He wondered what it felt like for her. Was her heart pounding? Her pulse sprinting? Was she aroused? Did she feel that pull of desire?

He did.

With a tiny lick of her lips that was nearly his undoing, Monica raised her chin and kissed him. It was soft and sweet. And an invitation.

"Monica?" he asked, heady with desire, but his voice deep and soft as he sought clarity.

"Kiss me," she whispered against his lips, hunger in her voice.

"Shit," Gabe swore before he gave in to the temptation of her and dipped his head to press his mouth down upon hers.

And it was just a second more before her lips and her body softened against him as she opened her mouth and welcomed him with a heated gasp that seemed to echo around them. The first touch of his tongue to hers sent a jolt through his body, and he clutched her closer to him as her hands snaked up his arms and then his shoulders before clutching the lapels of his tux in her fists. He assumed she was holding on while giving in to a passion that was irresistible.

Monica was lost in it all. Blissfully.

The taste and feel of his mouth were everything she ever imagined.

Ever dreamed of.

Ever longed for.

Don't miss what happens next in
One Night with Cinderella
by nationally bestselling author Niobia Bryant!

Available February 2021 wherever
Harlequin Desire books and ebooks are sold.

Harlequin.com

HDEXP0121

Introducing the
McKenzies of Ridge Trail,
an all-new sexy contemporary
romance series from
New York Times bestselling author

LORI FOSTER

"Storytelling at its best! Lori Foster should be on
everyone's auto-buy list."
—#1 *New York Times* bestselling author
Sherrilyn Kenyon on *No Limits*

Order your copy today!

SPECIAL EXCERPT FROM

Read on for a sneak peek at
No Holding Back,
book one in New York Times *bestselling author*
Lori Foster's exciting new contemporary romance
series, The McKenzies of Ridge Trail.

Available February 2021 from HQN Books!

Cade wanted to kick his own ass.

She'd been coming into the bar for months now. She hadn't yet given her name, but he knew it all the same. He made a point of knowing everyone in the bar, whether they were important to his operation or not.

Sterling Parson. Star for short.

Privately, he called her Trouble.

At a few inches shy of six feet, she walked with a self-possessed air that he recognized as more attitude than ability. She wore that swagger like a warning that all but shouted, "Back off."

The big rig she drove had *SP Trucking* emblazoned on the side, yet she was far from the usual trucker they got as customers.

The day she'd first walked in, heads had swiveled, eyes had widened and interest had perked—but after Cade swept his gaze around the room, everyone had gotten the message.

The lady was off-limits.

From the moment he'd first spotted Sterling, he'd sensed the emotional wounds she hid, knew she had secrets galore and understood she needed a place to rest.

She needed him.

Star didn't know that yet, but no problem. In his bar, in this shit neighborhood, he'd look out for her anyway—same as he did for anyone in need.

Moving to the window, he watched her leave. Her long stride carried her across the well-lit gravel lot, not in haste but with an excess of energy. He couldn't imagine her meandering. The woman knew one speed: full steam ahead.

She climbed into her rig with practiced ease. Head tipped back, she rested a moment before squaring her shoulders and firing the engine. She idled for a bit, then eased off the clutch and smoothly rolled out to the road. Cade watched until he couldn't see her taillights anymore.

Where she'd go, he didn't yet know—but he wanted to. He wanted to introduce himself, ask questions, maybe offer assistance.

Her preferences on that were obvious.

Except that tonight she'd watched him a little more.

Actually, she often noticed him, in a cautious, distrustful way. And she always came back.

Sometimes she'd sleep for an hour, sometimes longer. Tonight, she'd dozed for two hours before jerking awake in alarm.

A bad dream?

Or a bad memory?

If she kept to her usual pattern, she'd be back tomorrow night on her return trip. Maybe, just maybe, he'd find a chink in her armor. He glanced at the little table she always chose.

Tomorrow, he'd offer her something different.

Don't miss No Holding Back *by Lori Foster,*
available February 2021,
wherever HQN books and ebooks are sold.

HQNBooks.com

Copyright © 2021 by Lori Foster

PHLFEXP0221